Barry Spotter

Book One
(of two probably!)

The Beginning

A. M. Blank

**Grosvenor House
Publishing Limited**

This book is published by
Grosvenor House Publishing Ltd
28-30 High Street, Guildford, Surrey, GU1 3EL.
www.grosvenorhousepublishing.co.uk

A CIP record for this book
is available from the British Library

ISBN 978-1-908596-95-6

A story for boys and girls who do not usually read books and for some of those who do.

CHAPTER 1

The Notice

St. Gianeco Leapos Academy
Principal: **Professor George Clifford**

'A SPESHIALIST SCOOL FOR YUNG PEOPLE WHO WISH TO FOLLO A NON ACADEMIC CURRIQULUM WITH MANY DIFFERENT SUBJECTS AND LEADING TO A INTERESTING PROFESHION.'

Intervuws for any children aged 11, who are about to start secondary school will be held at this establishment (childrens home) next Tuesday 13th of July, 2011.

(Dislexics welcome)

Sine below if you would like to be intervuwed:

Sine here:

He stood.

He looked.

1

He read.

He moved on.

He returned.

He read.

He wondered.

He had never seen such a strange notice in his life. He had never seen such poor spelling, bad grammar and poor writing on an official notice before. At least, he assumed it was an official notice; after all, it was on the *'important notices for children'* board. He was checking the poor spelling and punctuation again and noticed the phrase 'dislexics wellcome', both words spelt wrongly! It was pretty clear that this was not a traditional school that was being advertised and, though it was called an Academy, it was not a very academic one. Still, that did not bother him so much. He was just deciding whether to put his name down for an interview, when he heard the voice he both knew and dreaded. A voice that held within it contempt, dislike, disgust, just about every 'dis' you can imagine.

'Hey, Spotter, what you looking at? What you trying to do, get away from me, your old mate?'

'Get lost, Useless,' said Barry, without looking away from the poster.

'How do you know it's me, Spotter?' said the voice.

'Because I can smell from 100 metres when someone has stepped in what dogs drop, Useless, now get lost,' said Barry.

'Now, little Spotter, you know you shouldn't use bad language to your olders and betters.'

'It's elders, not olders, you moron, and how can anyone be worse than you at anything?' said Barry.

'You know you are getting me annoyed now, Spotter. Be polite or I may visit you one of these nights and teach you some manners.'

'Sure, Useless, I'm shaking at the thought. Now get lost and let me read this in peace.'

'I will, young Baz, and don't forget my promise just now, I will be around to pay you a visit one of these nights and then we'll see how tough you really are.'

With a scary look, Useless Eustace, as he was called by everyone behind his back and to his face by one or two brave souls like Barry, walked back the way he had come leaving Barry to his quandary, to sign up for an interview to this weird place or not to. He decided to leave it a while; he had other things on his mind, like the visit the next day to the local comprehensive school, where he had a place waiting for him next year and where all his mates from the Home he lived in went to school when they passed eleven years of age.

CHAPTER 2

Getting to Know Barry

Barry Spotter lived in a children's home. A long time ago this Home would have been called an orphanage, and some older people in the local town still talked about the 'orphanage'. None of the children who shared this place with him had parents at all, or they had parents who could not or would not look after them. Barry never knew which was worse really: to have no parents at all that you know about, or to have parents you did know about, who did not, or could not bring you up. Of course, to say Barry didn't have parents was stupid. He had parents, he was not some alien or child conceived in a test tube. He was born naturally to a woman, his natural birth mother, and he definitely had a father. But he had never known either of them for one minute of his life that he could remember. Eleven years ago nurses had found him at a hospital entrance, with a label saying:

'THIS IS BARRY SPOTTER, PLEASE LOOK AFTER HIM.'

So the nurses had fed him, kept him warm and got him through the first dangerous days of life. Barry had not thrived and grown quickly; no, he had been a sick child and there were times in those first few weeks when he nearly did not make it. Two things had kept him alive.

The first was the care he received from all the doctors and nurses. They gave him twenty-four hour care and attention. Each time he sneezed, a nurse would be there to check on him in the glass box they kept him in, called an incubator. They fed him with liquids, they washed him and treated minor infections. They helped him to breathe and constantly kept an eye on his heart and other organs. They would just not consider losing this little baby. Something about him seemed special, even to these medical staff who saw and looked after babies every day of their lives.

The second thing that kept Barry, the newborn baby, alive was something the doctors call 'tenacity'. This they described as a sort of courage and unwillingness to give up. Something inside the little baby fought and struggled against all the odds and would not be beaten. Barry, aged eleven, still had this tenacity, or 'guts', as others called it. And he needed it every day of his life in the place where he lived, with the people who made up his world. Life for an eleven-year-old with no parents or family is never easy, but for Barry, it was harder than most.

He was thin, he had big ears that stuck out, and he had a strange eye. The coloured bit of the eye was mostly green, but it had a section of it that was a light brown or hazel colour. Between the green and the hazel there were black splodges, as if the black of the pupil was running into the iris or coloured bit of the eye. This, and his appearance generally, gave him a strange, some would say even weird, quality. This was especially true of people who met Barry for the first time.

Barry had always noticed the sort of strange looks people gave him when they first saw him, as if they were struggling to make sense of this gawky kid. All the time, and no matter how he tried (and he didn't very often), he could not look tidy. He was a scruffy kid. A thin, weird-looking, ugly kid and other kids never stopped letting him know it. To make it worse, he often had a runny nose, which dripped at the most awkward times and made him even more unappealing to look at. This was especially true if you were nearby having dinner or tea when his nose decided to gush! Breakfast was even worse; bacon, eggs and snot don't go well together. So Barry was not a popular child, which explained partly why he was still in the Home at the age of eleven.

Most babies, even older children, are adopted by people who want children because they can't have their own or by people who just want another child to add to their family. But whenever people looked at Barry, they could not help or hide their feelings of disgust; he just looked strange and he looked ugly and, as a result, first of all other babies, and then after that, other kids, were chosen by would-be parents. Barry was left in the children's home for another visit by other adults, and another rejection. By the age of seven, Barry was resigned to his fate; he even made his nose drip on purpose when adults gawped at him. Of course, these adults said nice things to Barry as they inspected him, but they could not hide their feelings from their eyes and their faces. Each visit by prospective parents just confirmed that Barry was a loser in life, would always live in children's home and never be chosen as someone's son. At least, until he became old enough to leave and get a flat, or a tent, or something of his own to live in. This was Barry's dream and he knew that it would be at least another six or seven years until he would even have a chance to do this.

The prospect of spending the next seven years in a Home and going to normal school, but having nothing to call your own, was depressing. No special room, no toys (these were all shared at the home), no brothers, no sisters, no parents, no grandparents, no uncles, no aunts. In short, nothing and no-one who belonged to him, and who he belonged to. It was an everyday reality, but it was a sad one, and Barry had to be 'tenacious' like the doctors said, just to survive.

CHAPTER 3

The Children's Home

The Home itself was a fairly grand old house. At least, it had been rather grand once upon a time. Now, it was rather worn and tired. It had high ceilings with fancy plaster work between them and the walls. The rooms tended to be large and, because it was so old and so large, it was often very cold in the winter. It was summer now, so the house was not cold and the massive iron radiators were switched off waiting for the colder months when they would blurp and clunk into operation and their impossible task of keeping the huge, cold, old house warm would begin. The rooms were dark from lack of light and also because the walls were painted or varnished in some dark brown colour.

Every room, except the bathrooms, was painted in this way. The bathrooms and toilets were pink plaster for the girls and pale blue plaster for the boys. These bare walls were usually covered in some kind of green moss. The sinks, baths and toilets were white and ancient, cracked and often not working properly. The bathrooms were all shared by four people from a dormitory. Barry shared his with his best friend, Raza, and two other younger boys, Philip and Sam.

The house had two sets of massive stairs and oak-covered walls in the corridors and halls, which would have been part of its *'grandeur'* once upon a time. The stairs were wide enough for four or five children to move up and down them at the same time. Most people visiting the orphanage would describe it as dark, cold and dismal.

The staff at the Home sometimes tried to improve things by hanging schoolwork on the walls, or using colourful posters to cover them. These attempts made the place look even worse. The posters and pictures made the house look more like a school, and a dark and dingy school at that. All in all, the house was grim. There was a reason for this. The children's home was run by a charity and they had rented or leased this large house for fifty years. During most of that time, repairs had been carried out and the building had been cared for. However, there were now only three years left on the lease and neither the owners nor the charity were prepared to spend money on the building any more. At the end of the three years, the house would be sold and the charity would have to find another property for the children to live in. The house provided a roof for the 'orphans', but the insides were crumbling and the exterior was being taken over by the ivy which climbed its walls.

There were adults who worked there to provide food, drink and clothes to wear, but it was really 'an institution', not a home, a proper home where children feel warm, cared for, loved and wanted. Barry summed it up when he spoke quietly at nights to his mate, Raza. He said, 'Raz, there is a world of difference between being liked and being loved. I know some people here like us, and they do their best for us, but when they go home they have their own children and they treat them differently. You can't say exactly how, but they <u>love</u> them, and they <u>like</u> us, if we are lucky.'

Some of the staff at the Home didn't even seem to like the children, never mind love them. The cook, Mrs. Dukes, was a spiky old woman, who cooked poor food and supplied small portions, so that the children were almost constantly hungry and looking for food in the form of sweets, cake or chocolate, anything to fill the empty feeling in their stomachs. She would shout at them if they left food of any sort, whether it was fat off the bacon in the morning or smelly, sweaty, over-cooked cabbage at night. Her cakes were the worst ever baked, dry and flat like 'frisbees' and often made with sour butter, which made them smell and taste dreadful. Even so, the need to eat usually saw these excuses for cakes demolished in a matter of seconds as the children fought for the biggest slices. Barry was thin, and he hated the food even more than most other children.

Even if you could stand her dreadful food, the woman herself was enough to make you feel sick. Her hair was long and straggly and always greasy. Her eyes followed the children everywhere with dark menace, just waiting for a fork to drop on the floor or one noisy bit of chewing; she forced the children to eat without making the slightest noise, saying it was,

'*Good manners that they needed to be taught and no mistake.*'

But, worst of all were her teeth. One of the big front teeth was missing completely, leaving a black hole, and the other was completely decayed and brown. It was like a rotting fang. The result of the rotten tooth at the front and her rotten teeth at the back was that her breath smelt like something had died in her mouth. Think of the worst smell you know – blue cheese, cow droppings, bad eggs, sweaty socks, whatever your worst smell is – and her breath was worse. Much worse! So, when she approached a child to tell them off, the child would try to turn their head away to avoid the smell of her breath. Then Mrs. Dukes would turn their heads around, and get even closer to the child to speak. Several children have been known to be sick on the spot as she shouted at them; others just managed to make it to the toilets and were sick there.

CHAPTER 4

Raza

Raza, or Hassan Raza, if you give him his full name, was Barry's best friend. In fact, best friend does not really do Raza justice. He was more than a best friend, he was like a brother, best friend, team-mate, soulmate all rolled into one. They knew each other so well and spent so much time together that they often knew what the other was thinking or going to say before they said it. Sometimes they did not even speak to understand each other; a look was often enough. Since Barry had seen the poster, he had been worried about bringing up the subject of leaving the Home, going to some weird school or 'academy' and ending their friendship. It was not going to be easy for either him or Raza and Barry doubted if Raza would understand how he could even think about doing it.

Barry was anxious as he approached his friend. He found Raza sitting on his bed in the dormitory. He was reading a book on Afghanistan, which is where he had been told he was born. Like Barry, Raza had never known his parents and he had been told that he had been brought to England as a baby. The story went that he

1 2

was probably smuggled into the country by some person who had found him in the rubble left from a bomb attack which had killed all his family. The truth was, no-one really knew how Raza came to be in England or, if someone did know, they were not sharing the information. So, like everyone at the children's home, he had never known the love of a parent or the warmth of a caring, loving family.

Unlike Barry though, Raza was handsome to look at. You don't normally use the word handsome when talking about young boys, but he was. He had olive brown skin, bright, dark brown eyes and black hair that glistened in all forms of light. His smile revealed neat white teeth and this smile just made everyone who saw it feel happy. He was small, but well proportioned. The most important thing about Raza though, was his intelligence. He was the brightest child in the Home, in the school and, Barry thought, probably the whole world. Not that Raza was a big-head or swot who showed off how much he knew. No, Raza's intelligence showed itself in the speed with which he learned things and how he was able to understand situations and solve problems.

Whenever Barry had a problem, something troubling him, stopping him from sleeping or making him a bit miserable, Raza would listen, think about it for a while and always, always come up with a solution. He was clever in other ways too. He seemed to know and understand what people were thinking, both adults and children. Raza worked people out. There was an air of mystery about Raza, he was different and very special.

He was always ready for Useless Eustace when he tried to frighten or humiliate the smaller children. Raza would defend the other children and almost always make Useless look stupid. Because of this, Useless Eustace hated Raza even more than he hated Barry and he wanted nothing more than to do something bad to them both. Useless was just waiting his time for the opportunity to get back at Barry and Raza for all the laughs they had enjoyed at his expense, and Useless knew that the opportunity was not far way. Useless had a plan, a good plan, and the two little 'brats', as he called them, would get their punishment and then he would be the one laughing.

Barry sat on the edge of Raza's bed. He was about to open his mouth, when Raza said, 'We'll both go.'

'What?' said Barry.

'We'll both go for an interview and, if we both like it, we will both go to the academy.'

'How did you know I was even thinking about it? I didn't say anything and I haven't signed up yet,' said Barry.

'No, but you will and so will I. So that's it, we both sign up and we both go for an interview,' replied Raza.

'Raza, why would you want to go to a school for idiots?'

'It's not for idiots, some of the most intelligent people in the world suffer from dyslexia, they just have a problem with reading and spelling. It doesn't mean they are thick!'

'I know that, Raz, but you are probably the brightest, most intelligent pupil in our school, this Home, for all I know, anywhere. So why would you go to a place which might not let you show just how clever you are?'

'Well, one reason is I'm not going to be split up from you, and the other is, I think there is something very interesting about this school, the poster and what they say about themselves,' said Raza.

'What do you mean interesting?'

'Think about it, Baz, who would write a poster like that, with spelling mistakes, the apostrophe missing from 'children's home', even dyslexia spelt wrongly?'

'I didn't know it was spelt wrong, but I'll take your word for it. So, who do you think is behind this poster and what type of school is '"Gianeco Leapos Academy"?' asked Barry.

'For once, Baz, I don't know. But I do know that it is a bit weird and I like finding out about weird things. So, we'll both go for an interview and we will both try and get to the bottom of this. Trust me, we will get to know more about it soon, and if we don't, well we had better get accepted so that we can find out more!'

'But, Raz, I'm not even sure I want to go yet,' said Barry.

'I know that, but that's what the interview and the visit to the comprehensive school tomorrow is all about. It will help us to make up our minds,' said Raza.

At that moment, as Raza finished his sentence, the bell for supper rang, so the two friends made their way down the massive staircase to the dining room to see what Mrs. Dukes had prepared with 'loving care' for them to eat before they went to bed. Tomorrow was a big day for Barry and Raza. They were due to visit the local comprehensive school, where there was a very special welcome being planned for them.

CHAPTER 5

Evening Meal

The dining room was already full and the children were standing behind their chairs waiting for Mr. Goodall, who was on duty for the night, to say Grace and allow the children to start to eat – if they could bear to eat what had been prepared for them.

The scraping of chairs and last bits of conversation died away and Mr. Goodall looked through his round, gold-rimmed glasses. He had long, curly hair that was best described as wild, a red complexion and a bit of a stammer when he spoke. He was a very kind man and all the children knew that they could trust him **most** of the time.

He began, 'F-F-F-For what we are a-a-a-about to receive, m-m-m-may the L-L-L-Lord make us truly thankful.' The last bit he rushed through, to avoid stammering any more.

As he finished, the noise began again as the children lifted grey metal covers to reveal what was in the food dishes. The clanging of the metal could not drown out the groans that left the children's mouths, as they looked in horror at Mrs. Dukes' supper.

Each table had three large serving dishes from which the older children, who acted as servers, gave out the food to the rest of the children sitting at the table. It was good to be server. On the odd day when the food was bearable, they could have larger portions, and on other days they could give big portions to the other children, who would struggle to get through the meal without being sick.

Today was a bad day. In one large dish there were large portions of tripe. Tripe is the lining of a cow's stomach, it is white-ish, looks like octopus skin, feels like rubber and, when cooked by Mrs. Dukes, tastes like it too. This tripe was swimming in a kind of fat and grease that smelt dreadful. In another dish were sprouts. These were not even cooked properly. They were cold, slimy and had rotten bits on them that most normal would people peel off before cooking. In the third dish was the only edible part of the meal. This was mashed potato. Even this was not nice, it had large lumps in it and black bits that would normally be taken out during peeling. Nevertheless, the potato was the bit that all the children went for first. The servers, of course, had larger portions of potato and hardly any of the other stuff. The children took small mouthfuls and chewed slowly, especially those who dared to try some of the sickly tripe. This would be another night, like most, when the children would go to bed hungry.

Barry and Raza shared glances and both knew and felt the disgust of the other children at the meal that was in front of them. They noticed Useless Eustace looking over at them. He had a horrible smile on his face and he shared a few words with the people next to him and laughed even more. He lifted his hands above the table and twisted them, as if he was wringing a pair of swimming trunks, then he took his finger and drew a line across his throat from ear to ear. He mouthed something across at Barry and Raza.

'What did the moron just say?' asked Barry.
Raza replied, 'He said, we're dead.'

They had heard threats like this from Useless before, but somehow the smile on his face was even more worrying than usual. Useless knew something that Barry and Raza did not.

The two friends replaced the lids on the serving dishes, finished the potato they had taken, stacked the plates and cutlery, then collected the cloth to wipe their table. The meal was over. It was time to get ready for the visit to the local comprehensive school tomorrow and get to bed. The feeling of an empty stomach was easier to bear in sleep. Mr. Goodall would come around and check on the dormitories at about nine o'clock and the children would settle down to sleep half an hour after that. Though they said nothing to each other, Raza and Barry both went to sleep wondering just what Useless had planned for them, and when and how he would try to get even.

CHAPTER 6

The Local Comprehensive School

Breakfast was always the best meal for the children at the Home, because they could eat as much cereal and milk and then toast and jam or marmalade, as they liked. The food was plain and simple and had not been ruined by Mrs. Dukes. The dining room was much quieter at breakfast too and, for most children, it was a good start to the day.

After breakfast, Barry and Raza along with two girls, who were also due to start at Moorlake Comprehensive in the September, went around the back of the house to where the minibus was parked. Written boldly along both sides of the bus was the name 'Freeman's Children's Home'. The writing left no-one in any doubt about where this bus was from and who was inside it. Sometimes, as the bus went along the streets, other children would make signs at the children in the bus and shout dirty words and phrases at them. For some reason, these 'normal' children felt that children from the Home were not as good as themselves and that they should be made fun of and abused. It was not safe for children from the Home to walk in the local town in groups. They were often picked on or pushed around. Sometimes they were spat at and regularly called names. So, with this in mind, the children would have preferred to travel to the high school in a bus which did not have the name of the Home all over the side, but that was not to be.

The visit to the local comprehensive school was part of what their primary school called 'induction'. These visits were meant to help the children get used to the idea that they would soon be moving schools, and to help them to overcome any fears they might have about it. The teachers at the comprehensive – or high school, as it was referred to – did some interesting lessons with their visitors and told them how exciting life at the new, bigger, better school would be. Not many of the children were fooled by these visits. They knew that when they started school properly the following September, the same teachers would be far less entertaining and far more strict. It was all smiles during induction visits but then when school started properly, out would come the boring text books, the maths books, the homework. Teachers would suddenly have scary looks and threats for those children who did not do exactly as they were told.

Moorlake Comprehensive School was no different to thousands of other schools around England. The fact that it received children from a children's home as well as children from more normal backgrounds, did not change anything much.

The journey to the high school was uneventful. None of the children spoke. They all sat quietly and kept their thoughts to themselves. These were not happy thoughts.

Older children in the Home passed on stories of previous visits. Stories which told of having their heads pushed down toilets, or being insulted and bullied in other ways. Induction visits for the children from the children's home were rarely pleasant affairs and today's visit would turn out to be no different.

When they arrived at the school gates, there were hundreds of young people making their way up the drive. As some of these noticed the writing on the bus, the shouting began from some of the older and bigger high school pupils.

'Go back home!' shouted one big lad, and then added, 'Oh, I forgot, you don't have a home, you're orphans!' He laughed and some of his friends joined in the joke.

Some of the other young people did not see this as funny at all. They just looked ashamed to be associated with such cruel and bad-mannered bullies. Other bad things were shouted, and Barry and Raza looked at each other. The look they shared said it all. This was not how they wanted to spend the next seven years, being ridiculed, bullied, laughed at and probably made to feel inferior and worthless.

At the top of the drive, Mr. Goodall stopped the minibus and let the children out. He was upset by what he had heard, but then he had heard it all before. It hurt him to see the children from the Home treated so badly, but he knew that there was very little that he could do to prevent it; sometimes by trying to help, adults just made things worse for the children. Still, he felt sad and a little ashamed that he could not protect the children in his care from such abuse. He led the four children into the main entrance, where they joined in with other children from their primary school who had been brought by their parents, or some who had walked by themselves for their first visit to what was to be their new school.

All of the visiting children waited in the main reception area until the headteacher of the school came to greet them.

Mrs. Granger, the headteacher, was a small, quite fat lady. Her dark grey jacket and skirt matched and, with a white blouse underneath, she looked very smart and very strict. As she approached the visiting primary school children, she somehow just looked very important and a bit scary. She eventually stopped about three metres from the group. Then the strangest thing happened. Her face lit up, her eyes smiled at the children and she immediately had their attention. Suddenly she no longer looked scary but, instead, very friendly and warm. You could almost sense a change in the atmosphere. The worried looks on the faces of the children disappeared and turned to smiles, aimed at the woman who would soon be their new headteacher.

'Well, hello to you all,' said Mrs. Granger.
    'We have been looking forward to your visit for some time and we have planned a very exciting day for you. At least, I hope you will find it exciting,' she said.
    'As you know, all the staff at Moorlake are here to help you and to make feel at home, so do not hesitate to ask for anything you want. We all want you to leave here

today very keen and eager to return in September, when you will become part of the Moorlake family. My name is Mrs. Granger and I am the headteacher here. At the end of the day, I will meet with you all again and you can tell me about the best bits of the day, and you can ask me any questions then about this coming September. Now, I will leave you in the capable hands of my staff. Good morning.'

And right on key, as they had been told to do at their primary school, the children all said together,

'Thank you, and good morning, Mrs. Granger.' This was said in that sickly way that children all have to say 'Good morning everybody' in school assemblies. It is a bit like a singing style that everyone must join in with, even if it makes them feel stupid. Mrs. Granger smiled, turned and left the group of children.

As she made her way to her office, she smiled to herself, because once again the children had been *programmed* to say their little speech all together and all in that sickly primary school-style. She would soon 'knock' all that sort of rubbish out of them in September. Mrs. Granger was a good actress. She could play the part of the generous, pleasant, kind person perfectly and she knew that by the end of the day all the visitors would be fooled and keen to choose her school before any of the others in the area. Then, once they were in the school properly in September, she could show them just what a strict headteacher she really could be. She could hardly wait!

At this stage, several other high school teachers appeared and they all chose five or six of the children and led them on a tour of the school. The children were shown the gymnasium, the swimming pool, the science laboratories, the technical workshops, food technology room and all the special facilities that the school had.

The tour left Barry and Raza unsure of what to make of this school. The specialist classrooms and laboratories were great and they did look exciting compared with the facilities at their little primary school, but the normal classrooms looked dull and untidy. There was nothing on the walls to liven the place up and no evidence of children's work. Their primary school classroom was always decorated brightly and loads of work on the walls showed parents, and anyone else visiting the school, just what the children had been learning.

As they left the biology laboratory, which was fascinating with all the stuffed animals and body parts in jars, Barry asked Raza what he thought of the place.

Raza replied, 'The labs look amazing! The workshops have loads of equipment too. It's very different to our school! What do you think, Baz?'

Barry was not as enthusiastic.

'I have a strange feeling about this place. It just does not seem real to me somehow. I wonder what it's like to be here every day?'

'The same as any other school I suppose, Baz, some good and some bad lessons. Studying what other people think is interesting rather than what you want to study, preparing for examinations, and doing exactly what teachers tell you to do. Nothing changes in school, Barry, and for us, nothing is going to change unless **we** do something about it.'

Barry looked at his friend, he knew that he was referring the interviews for St. Gianeco's Academy and he knew that Raza was right. It had to be worth an interview at least. If Barry had any doubts at all, they were about to be removed.

The bell rang and the teachers took the children to the dining room for lunch. They were given first choice of the food, told to sit where they liked to eat, and then to go into the school playground for the rest of the lunch break. The food was quite good, there was pizza, chips, salad, various puddings. Compared to Mrs. Dukes' awful food, it was delicious and, for once, there was plenty of it!

As Barry and Raza were finishing their meal, they looked around and saw something they would rather not have seen. Useless Eustace was sitting at a table nearby with some very big, very rough-looking boys. They all had their eyes on Barry and Raza while Useless was telling them things, and they all nodded their heads, as if understanding exactly what Useless was talking about. Barry and Raza took their trays to the counter. They did not look towards Useless and his gawping cronies. Raza and Barry were not stupid, they knew when it was wise to look away from people. They did not want any trouble with Useless here. Here, Useless held the upper hand.

They went to a quiet part of the playground. Both boys had a feeling of dread. They did not know exactly how and when it would happen, but Useless had been threatening them for some time. The look on his face had suggested that today just might be the day he lived up to his threats and took some revenge on Barry and Raza.

Both boys were determined to stick together, no matter what happened. And then it did begin to happen!

First, a rope appeared from nowhere. It circled Barry and Raza and then tightened, trapping them together and holding them firm, so that they could not move. Then, from around the corner, came Useless and four other boys, big boys, rough boys. The fifth, who was a giant for his age, held the rope tight.

'Hey, young Raza and Baza, fancy meeting you here!' This was Useless speaking, and though his voice was joyful and playful, this did not show in his eyes. His eyes were full of menace.

Useless had waited a long time for this moment and he was going to enjoy it to the full. The group of big boys formed a circle around the two trapped friends, and their faces held exactly the same message as Useless'. That message was the promise of pain and trouble.

Useless moved. He took hold of one of Barry's ears. He twisted it so that the skin at the bottom almost tore. Barry squirmed with pain, but made no sound. He would not give Useless the benefit of knowing how much it hurt.

'Brave little boy, aren't we, Baz? Can take the pain, can't we, Baz?'

Then he punched Barry in the stomach with such force that everyone could hear the air gasp out of him. Even if Barry wanted to speak now, he couldn't; he had no breath to do so. Useless then grabbed his hair and yanked his head up. He slapped Barry across the face and then asked,

'What's my name, young Baz?'

26

He paused, waiting for the answer, which Barry could not give because he could not breathe.

'Who is the boss at our house, young Baz?' And he slapped his face again, the force twisting Barry's head.

Blood began to mix with snot on Barry's face, and a small trickle began to form at the side of his mouth.

'Leave him, you scumbag!' shouted Raza. 'You are just a thick, brainless bully, Useless. Let us go!'

'Oooh,' said all the thugs together. 'We have a hero amongst us. Little Raza, clever little Raza!'

The thugs laughed and then one stepped in and grabbed Raza by the throat. Raza struggled and kicked out but it was useless, the tormentor towered above the tiny Raza.

'Listen, little orphan, we don't like your sort at our school, you bring the place down. Eustace here, he's like one of us. He has parents, he has proved himself. Kids like you are like dung and you smell like it. You and your ugly little pal here will get this treatment every day, and on some days worse, if you come here in September. So don't. Go somewhere else!'

Then with a sick smile he said, 'No, on second thoughts, do come here, because I will get great pleasure out of beating you to pulp every day. You know, doing my bit for society.'

He looked at the rest of the gang. They all smiled back at him, nodded their heads and shouted,

'Yer, that's right, Macka. Give it to 'em every day. It will be our play time. Almost werf comin' to school for!'

Useless, told one of the other thugs to tie Barry's and Razza's shoelaces together.

'Make a good job of it, you know, plenty of knots for our little boys to untie!'

One of the other boys knelt down and began tying.

The rope was loosened. Useless gave Barry one more slap across the head and then he and his mates left the two friends.

As the thugs left, other children in the playground could see Barry and Raza for the first time since their ordeal had begun. Some gasped in horror, others laughed as the two friends struggled to take their shoes off. Barry, for the first time, began to have tears in his eyes and his whole body began to jerk as he fought back the tears. Raza put his arm around his friend's shoulders and moved around in front of him, so that no-one could see Barry's sobs. Raza, too, had tears in his eyes, but these were tears of anger.

'This is not finished, Barry. Useless will pay for this, trust me.'

The two managed to sit on the tarmac and undo the knots that held their shoes together. When their feet were released, the two friends began to get themselves together.

'I need the toilet,' said Barry. 'I think I wet myself when he hit me.'

'Come on, Baz, this way,' said Raza, and he led his friend to the toilets. Here they washed their faces and straightened their clothes as best they could. Barry looked pale and the marks of the slaps on his face were still visible. Inside his stomach was churning and he felt close to being sick.

The rest of the afternoon passed uneventfully. The children watched a science lesson and Mrs. Granger came with her polished smile to say goodbye to them all. She reminded them of the need to come back in September fresh and ready to learn.

She looked at Barry's swollen, red face and was just about to say something. Then she thought better of it. It was not a good idea in front of the other children. She did not want to say anything that might put them off coming back in September.

Not even the two girls in the minibus asked him how he had come to get the bruises which were just beginning to form on his face by the time they returned to the home. Perhaps people were not surprised that boys sometimes looked a little worse for wear, or perhaps they just could not be bothered to ask.

Mr. Goodall noticed something was wrong with Barry.

'Are you OK, Barry?' He could see that Barry had marks on his face.

'I'm OK, thanks, Sir, I just took a few knocks playing football at dinner time.' He stole a quick look at Raza which said,

'Don't say anything. Don't make it worse!'

Mr. Goodall knew something was not quite right, but he decided to let it go. He had tried in the early days to do something about it. Now he just accepted that bullying was a fact of life. Something the children from the 'Home' had to learn to handle and overcome.

Raza did not agree, he knew that Mr. Goodall was just taking the easy way out and being weak. He also knew that adults were not perfect, even pretty decent adults like Mr. Goodall behaved badly sometimes.

CHAPTER 7

The Decision

Barry and Raza sat on Barry's bed. The pain in his stomach had gone and his face was now just bruised, not red and swollen. Inside he still felt strange.

When you have been hurt, abused in some way, the feeling inside is like having butterflies in your stomach, but not good ones. They keep fluttering around, letting you know that you are not right, and that what happened was not right. You fear going to sleep because you know that what you have suffered may visit you again in your dreams and you will suffer it all over again.

At times like these, you need love, you need care, and most kids get it from their parents. In Barry's case, he was unlucky not to have parents. But he was the luckiest kid in the world to have Raza as his best friend.

'Baz, it's a simple decision. We don't want to go back to that school in September, do we?'

'No, definitely not,' said Barry.

'Right, so we have to go for an interview for St. Gianeco's, and we have to do our best to get a place there. Whatever it is like and wherever it is, has to be better than where we have been today. I don't care how badly written the notice was. It is our escape. It gets us away from Useless and his mates at Moorlake,' said Raza.

'I know you are right, Raz, and we do have to go for it. I just worry about what will happen if we don't both get in,' said Barry.

'That's easy,' said Raza, 'it's both of us or neither of us, we do not get separated.'

CHAPTER 8

The Interviews

Eventually, Tuesday the 11th of July arrived. Barry and Raza were the only people who had put their names down for an interview. Other children had read the notice, of course, but for them the spelling and bad punctuation suggested that St. Gianeco Leapos Academy was not a very good school at all, and no-one at the Home had any information on the place either.

Searches on the internet revealed nothing. Not surprisingly, staff at the Home warned the children off going for an interview, and secretly they wondered if there was something not quite right, something that did not make sense about St. Gianeco Leapos Academy and the interviews that were about to take place.

For Barry and Raza, it was the only option. For them, the future was bleak at Moorlake and so was the future at the Home. It was worth a try, and if no-one else was applying, they stood a good chance, didn't they? It was then that they met Mr. Goodall outside the dining room.

'Morning, lads,' he said.

'Morning, Mr. Goodall,' the friends replied. 'Er, Mr. Goodall, do you know anything about the St. Gianeco place?'

Mr. Goodall replied, 'Not much, Raza. They come here about once every seven years and interview people, but they have never accepted anyone from here before and this is the third time they have been since I have worked here.'

'So, how many children have applied before?' asked Barry. He was now getting worried. His assumption that because there were only two of them applying, it would be easy to get accepted, was looking a bit shaky.

'Oh, let me see,' said Mr. Goodall. 'About six the first time and five the second.'

'That means eleven altogether have applied and none were accepted! That's bad for us,' said Raza.

'Oh, it's much worse than that, Raza. They interview all over England; almost every children's home in the country is visited for just a few places once every six or seven years. I have heard that they interview several thousand children throughout the year and they only have about twenty places to fill, so it is a very selective place, difficult to get into. The truth is, no-one knows how they choose their pupils. It is not just cleverness or sporting ability. You will soon see. They have their own tests and trials, so be prepared and do your best.'

Barry and Raza looked at each other. Some chance they had! One place at St. Gianeco would be remarkable; for two of them to be accepted, it would be a miracle!

'By the way, Barry, the oth, oth, other, d-d-day at the school…' Mr. Goodall stammered.

'It's alright, Mr. Goodall, I know there was nothing that you could do,' said Barry.

Of course there was, and Mr. Goodall knew it and he was ashamed of himself for not standing up for Barry in the face of violence and bullying. He smiled a weak smile and wished the boys good luck.

Within a few minutes, as the boys were beginning to lose heart and confidence, they saw an enormous vehicle enter the gates of the children's home. It was like an enormous coach, bus, horsebox and mobile library all rolled into one – it was a *'wonder bus'*. It was all black with gleaming chrome wing mirrors and bumpers. The windows were blacked out and on the side was written,

'ST. GIANECO LEAPOS ACADEMY'

in very smart grey letters. If the original notice that Barry had read looked cheap, nasty and badly written, this vehicle looked just the opposite. It looked very expensive and classy. The bus had lots of antennae and aerials on its roof.

As the vehicle passed them and came to a halt in front of the old house, Barry and Raza looked at each other, both smiled and shook hands. They both thought the same thing. **This was going to be their day!**

After about fifteen minutes, a small, grey-haired, immaculately dressed man came into the house. He smiled at the two boys and went straight to Mr. Goodall's office. He was there no longer than five minutes before he returned to the hall where the boys were waiting.

'Good morning,' he said. 'I assume that you are Barry, Barry Spotter, and that you are Raza, Hassan Raza?' He held out his hand and shook both boys' hands with his right hand, Barry first and then Raza.

He was very small; he was not that much taller than Barry. He had the brightest blue eyes that either boy had ever seen. His dark blue suit and waistcoat looked like new and fitted him perfectly. His silver, grey hair was swept back over his head and his teeth gleamed as he smiled. The most striking feature was his silver moustache, which had sharp points at each end where they had been twisted and smoothed into shape. The boys had never seen anyone so smart and impressive in all their lives, and both fell, immediately, under his charming spell.

'I am Professor George Clifford, the director of the St. Gianeco Leapos Academy. I will helping to interview you today and I think the sooner we start the better. I know you two are inseparable, Mr. Goodall has just told me what great friends you are, but for this interview we need to see you by yourselves. So, who is going to come first?'

Neither of the boys wanted to be pushy and they were in danger of never making the decision at all, when Professor Clifford helped them out.

'Who put their name up first on our poster?'
    'I did,' said Barry.

'Good, then you can come first, Barry. Raza, I suggest that you go to your room or something. This usually takes about two hours.' He smiled with genuine kindness as he spoke, and something about his tone made the boys feel as if he liked them already. Something about him made them feel that he knew them. He did not treat them like children, but more like young people who were both intelligent and mature.

Raza shook Barry's hand.
'Good luck, Baz,' he said.
Barry and Professor Clifford made their way to the big black vehicle, the 'Wonder Bus'.

As Barry entered the vehicle, he could hardly believe his eyes. Inside there was gymnasium equipment, running machines and rowing machines, all sorts of physical testing equipment. Alongside these were screens and monitors, all showing different types of information, readings and graphs. In one corner were two people in white laboratory coats, and behind them was a special kiosk, about twice the size of a phone box. Inside this was a table with headphones on it, and two screens attached to the wall.

It was like something out of a space station, or rocket command centre, and it did not fill Barry with confidence. He had never seen anything like it before. Barry noticed that there was a small door at the far end of the room leading to the rest of the 'Wonder Bus'. What he could see was very impressive, but it was only about half of the total length of the vehicle and what was beyond this other door was a mystery.

After he had introduced Barry to the two people in white laboratory coats, George Clifford disappeared through this door. And it was clear that whatever lay behind it, was not for the eyes of those being tested. It was secret and out of bounds.

The two people in laboratory coats introduced themselves using first names only. The man was called Russell and the woman, Nina. Nina spoke first.

'OK, Barry, what we need first are your fingerprints and a DNA sample.' 'What?' thought Barry. The only people who he had heard about needing tests like that were criminals. Was he mixing with criminals?

'It's OK, Barry, we do this to build up a file on you, so that we will never lose you! These tests tell us something unique about you, that no-one else could ever copy. So, no matter where you go or what you do, we will always know our Barry Spotter!'

Barry knew there was no way back and, to be fair, Russell and Nina looked more like scientists to him than criminals, so he placed both his hands on a special screen on a table, a light flashed and that was the fingerprinting done; none of the old-fashioned ink pads and paper. Next, Nina took a cotton wool stick or swab and scraped the inside of his cheek. That was the DNA test done. Finally, Russell took a special camera and took a picture of Barry's eyes. He said this was to look carefully at the iris or coloured bit of his eye, which is also unique to every person.

Nina then took out a stethoscope and listened to his chest and back.

'No problems there, Barry. Fit as a fiddle, I'd say.' And she smiled a lovely smile as she said it. Barry was beginning to enjoy all this attention.

Next it was Russell's turn.

'Right then, Barry, we have two sorts of tests for you now. The first tests are mental tests and for that you will go into the kiosk there and follow the instructions that are given to you on the screens and through the headphones. Are you ready for this? Do you want a drink or something before we start?'

'No thanks, I am ready, I think,' said Barry rather timidly. He entered the kiosk, put on the headphones and concentrated on the screens. The first questions were maths questions – simple calculations – and Barry found them all easy. This gave him confidence. Next there were written questions which he had to read, understand and then answer by speaking through the mouthpiece.

After these came strange questions asking him to find identical shapes or find the odd ones out, solve sequences of letters and numbers. These were much harder and, after about half an hour of the gruelling testing, Barry began to sweat.

Still the questions came.

'If A is worth 1 and C is worth 3, what is the value of the '*tenpence*'?' Barry started to calculate.

'*t*' must be worth 20 and '*e*' must be worth 5.

Then he stopped, smiled and wrote the word, *tenpence* using the keyboard.

Well done! flashed the screen.

More and more of these questions came at him and then, after exactly forty-five minutes, the screens went black and the door to the kiosk opened. There, with a drink of orange juice and a biscuit, were both Russell and Nina, both smiling and telling him that he had done well.

'Wow!' said Barry. 'I've never done anything like that before.'

'Did you enjoy it?' asked Russell.

'Well, I don't know if I enjoyed it, but I did get a buzz from it. I just wanted to keep going and thinking of answers that were not always the obvious ones. Yes, I think I did enjoy it. Is that the sort of thing we do at the academy?'

Russell and Nina smiled at each other.

'Well, sort of, yes. St. Gianeco Leapos is very different. We don't do the normal things that schools do and we don't often do traditional subjects, but it is exciting and challenging and sometimes slightly weird!'

All three laughed at this and Barry finished his drink.

'OK, Barry, that's your brain exercised, now it's time for your body,' said Nina.

She pointed to a screen that he could go behind, with a wall which had pegs on it. In some boxes on the floor were new trainers of various sizes, running shorts and vests.

'Just get changed into a running kit that fits you best and come out when you are ready.'

Barry found some size five trainers, a blue vest and matching shorts. When he came out from behind the screen, he looked like an athlete; a skinny, bony, awkward athlete, but nonetheless, an athlete.

'Barry, we want you to go on the running machine here and to run so that you stay in the middle of the running pad.'

Nina placed some sticky pads onto his chest and legs and one on his head, and then told him to slowly start to walk and then run faster as the speed of the running machine increased.

'We will control the speed, and the pads on your body will send information to our computers over there. If you want to stop at any time, just raise your hand and we will stop the machine immediately. If you feel dizzy or sick, stop us straight away. Ok?'

Barry nodded and began to move his legs and feet. Gradually the runway began to move more and more quickly. Nina watched intently as Barry worked harder and harder to keep pace with the machine. Russell was busy watching the computer screen over to the right. After fifteen minutes, both Russell and Nina looked very concerned. Nina went to increase the speed but, before she did, she checked with Russell whose eyes were glued to the computer screen, taking in all the readings and data on Barry's body. He nodded and she increased the speed, Barry just increased his pace. After a few minutes, this was repeated and again and again the speed was increased and Barry, though clearly working very hard, managed to keep pace.

Eventually, after thirty-five minutes, Nina and Russell shared a nod and began to slow the speed down.

Eventually the machine and the noise stopped.

'Remarkable, Barry,' said Nina, 'quite remarkable!'

Barry said nothing for a minute then smiled and said, 'Enjoyed that too!'

Again all three laughed. This had been one of the best mornings that Barry could remember. He felt as if he had been tested to his limits both mentally and physically and he had enjoyed it; he had loved it!

'Right then, Barry, that's all the testing done, we have everything we need now. You will just have a short interview with Professor Clifford and that is it, you are finished! You have done well,' said Russell.

'When will I know if I have been accepted?' asked Barry.

'We generally let you know, through Mr. Goodall, by the end of the day, but Professor Clifford will tell you more about that soon, Good luck, Barry. It's been fun meeting you. You are quite a special boy!'

Russell and Nina disappeared through the little door to the secret room behind, and Professor Clifford came out.

'Better get changed again,' said the principal, 'and then we can have our interview on the move. I think better when I'm walking. How about you, Barry?

'I don't know sir, but I would like some fresh air after all that running.'

'Yes, indeed you probably would!' said Professor Clifford with a smile.

'How do you think the tests went?' asked Professor Clifford with a twinkle in his eye.

'I don't know really, Sir. They were not like any tests I've done before, so it's hard to judge.'

'Well,' said the professor, 'they are looking at your results as we speak, so that we can tell you the result as soon as possible. But I am more interested in other things just now, Barry. Can I ask you a few questions when you are changed?'

'Of course, Sir,' said Barry and he went and changed into his normal clothes. Both of them began a slow walk around the gardens.

'Well, Barry, Gianeco Leapos Academy is a long way from here, do you think you would miss your friends here at the Home? After all, you have spent most of your life here, have you not?'

'All of my life, Sir, that I can remember anyway. I won't miss much, Sir. The food is pretty awful, the house is old and damp and cold in winter, and I only have one real friend.'

'Of course, young Raza. How would you cope without him, Barry?'

'I wouldn't, Sir. I could not go anywhere without Raza, we are more than friends; more like brothers, Sir.'

'I see,' said the Professor. 'So if Raza passes the test and you don't, do you think he would say the same thing, Barry?'

'I know he would, Sir, we have already agreed it.'

'And you trust him to stick to his word, do you?' The professor said this in a way to test Barry's trust in his friend and this annoyed Barry a bit. So the next time Barry spoke there was a just a little bit of anger in his voice.

'If you doubt that, Sir, you don't know Raza or me very well. We would never cheat on each other, or let each other down. That's the way it has been since we first met.'

'OK, Barry, I was only trying to test you a little, I already understand your loyalty and deep friendship with Raza. It does put us in a bit of a pickle though. I'll be honest with you. We have interviewed thousands of children for the academy over the last two years and your Home is the last one that we have to visit. Soon we have to choose just twenty children from the thousands that we have tested and interviewed. In the history of St. Gianeco Leapos, we have never, ever selected two children from the same place before. So I have to say that it is very unlikely that both of you will be selected. I know this may seem hard, Barry, but, like you, I want to be completely honest.'

'Thank you, Sir,' said Barry, 'I understand, and though I was beginning to like the idea of coming to your academy, I like Nina and Russell and you, Sir, but if that's the way it is, I will just have to settle for Moorlake Comprehensive.'

'Well, let's see how the tests go, Barry. I know that you would fit in at St. Gianeco's and I know that you would love it.'

They had returned to the front of the house and were shaking hands to say goodbye. Barry could not help but feel disappointed. The more he heard about St. Gianeco Leapos Academy and the more he met the people from there, especially this wise and honest professor, the more he really wanted to go there and to get away from this home and the prospect of Moorlake School.

'Well, goodbye for now, Barry, I've enjoyed talking with you. Maybe we will meet again, you never know,' said the professor.

'Goodbye, Sir, say goodbye to Russell and Nina for me please, and good luck, Sir, with the choosing, I mean.'

'Yes, Barry, very wise, we should never underestimate the impact of luck on our lives. One little event can change everything, sometimes in the most unpredictable way. Oh, and by the way, your running test, Barry. Your result was the highest we have ever measured for fitness and endurance; very special for such a skinny kid, if you don't mind me saying so!'

And with that they parted, Barry to his dormitory and the professor to the '*Wonder Bus*'. As the professor made his way to the secret room, he noticed Raza in the special kiosk with Nina and Russell looking on. They both looked completely astonished; their mouths drooping open in disbelief. The professor smiled to himself, twisted one side of his pointed, silver moustache with his fingers and made his way through the door.

CHAPTER 9

The Results of the Tests

In the secret room at the back of the '*Wonder Bus*' the activity was hectic. People were busy taking sheets from printers, checking screens, making telephone calls and having animated discussions. The whole room was full of busy people, some in white coats, some with headphones on and others straining their eyes to read papers, screens, graphs and tables full of data. In the middle of the room was a large round table with about 10 chairs available.

The professor sat on one of these chairs, tweaked his moustache and, after a few moments of thought, suddenly brought all the activity to a halt. He simply pressed a small button under the table and all the screens went blank, all the noise stopped abruptly and all the white-coated technicians, and those people in normal clothes, came to the table. Some sat on the chairs and others stood behind them. All eyes were on Professor George Clifford as he spoke. From the noisy activity to total silence took something like five seconds. The professor suddenly took on a new and even more impressive level of importance. If there was any doubt about who was in charge of this operation, it had now been removed in seconds. When he spoke it was with absolute authority and everyone listened intently.

'Thank you, everyone,' he said. 'We have some important things to discuss and information to consider. I hope that you are all prepared and ready.'

Some nodded, others just looked nervously around, obviously hoping that they were properly prepared and that they had the answers that the professor wanted.

'Anthony, first can we discuss the Spotter boy? **Is he the one we were looking for?**'

A very intelligent but nervous-looking man in a white coat replied in a somewhat shaky voice.

'Yes, sir, no doubt about it. The DNA fits, the finger-prints match and the iris test confirms that he is the one we were looking for. It is him. In fact, we did not need to do the iris test, sir. Did you notice his left eye with the two colours and black discolouration of the iris? This is an identical genetic match to his father, sir!'

'Yes, Anthony, I did. You forget that I knew the boy's father very well,' he paused, 'very well indeed! Barry's name was also a big clue for us, and his age of course.'

The professor allowed himself a moment or two to reflect on this fact, before his next question was out.

'His mental or cognitive tests. Results, Jane?'

A small, fair-haired woman in her early twenties replied.

'As we might have predicted, sir, given the data we have on his parents, excellent spatial awareness, very high logic reading, not so hot on mathematics, but workable and suitable for our programmes. Overall, he is an excellent candidate, from a cognitive point of view.'

Outside in the testing area, amazing things were happening in the kiosk which Russell and Nina could hardly believe. The professor knew nothing of this as he continued.

The professor went to his moustache again.
'And physical, James, what is the lowdown on that?'

'As I told you before you left, sir, his stamina and VO2 results are the highest we have recorded since our records began. He has very little muscle as yet, and his diet has not been good here at the Home, sir, and he is only eleven. But it is likely that he will develop along similar lines to his father, and his mother was a very impressive physical specimen too, I believe.'

The professor's eyes smiled at the memory.

'Yes indeed, she was very impressive, James,' he said.
    'So, people, we have found the one we were specif-ically looking for and that would seem to wrap up the selection for this year. Well done to you all, I believe we have a very special group of students coming to us this year and I have a feeling that with this last selection, young Barry, we have the strongest group we have had for a very long time. Only time will tell if our selection methods have worked again, and of course the work that we will all put in over the next seven years will also determine the measure of our success.'

The professor was about to say thank you again and break up the meeting when Nina and Russell entered the room. Their eyes were agog with excitement. The professor could see that they were dying to tell everyone in the room about Raza.

'Sir,' said Russell. 'We have just tested probably,' he paused, 'no definitely, the brightest, most promising child that we have ever tested! On all intelligence counts, he goes off the scale. He completed all, yes all, the questions in under thirty-five minutes; the previous record was forty-five minutes. Quite frankly, sir, he is an absolute genius!'

The professor took all this information in without showing any emotion or excitement. He coolly tried to make sense of what was being said and to work out what could be done.

'Anthony, DNA. Where is he from?' the professor barked.
    'Unusual, sir, obviously Middle East, possibly Iraq, maybe somewhere else, but no direct record or link for us to be sure.'
    This was most unusual, and the fact was not lost on George Clifford.

'No record, eh?' the professor's moustache got the treatment again.
    'So, he may have something in his background that is a bit special. But people, we are wasting our time. We have our twenty children, do we not? There is no point in deliberating. I think we should recall the Spotter boy and offer him a place. If he declines because of his loyalty

to his friend, we can offer a place to this remarkable enigma, Raza and see if he is as loyal as his friend expects him to be.'

'But, sir,' this was James, 'we hoped to find Barry, he was the only boy we set out to find. The others have qualified through their ability, but we always hoped to locate Barry.'

'Indeed, James, it's all a ploy. When Barry discovers that his friend Raza would indeed let him down, he is sure to change his mind about coming on his own, and then we will have our twentieth and very special pupil!'

This was a sneaky side of the professor that was rarely seen by anyone, and it was not a very pleasant plan. To separate and split two best friends and to invite them to be disloyal was not a very good or decent thing to do. The people in the room showed this on their faces, especially Nina and Russell, who had met the boys and had immediately liked them both.

CHAPTER 10

The Offer of a Place

Both boys were sitting on Barry's bed when Mr. Goodall approached them and said, 'Right then, Barry, you are first. Can you go back to the bus? It appears that they are going to let you know today, as this is the last of the interviews for this year. Good luck, Barry, if this is what you want. They seem a weird bunch to me, but what do I know!'

Barry looked at Raza, they both knew how much Barry wanted a place at this strange, but exciting school. Barry made his way to the bus and entered the part where the test had taken place. All the screens and machinery had been turned off and the place felt very different to earlier in the day.

At a small table were Nina, Russell and the professor.

'Well, hello again, Barry,' said the professor. 'Take a seat and let's have a little chat.

'The good news is we have a place for you at St. Gianeco Leapos Academy this September. Before you accept or reject the offer, we would like to show you some of the things we do at the academy and to listen to some of our past pupils who have just finished with us this year, after seven years of what we call an alternative education. If you will, Russell.' He nodded at Russell.

Russell stood and went to a screen with a DVD player below it. He flicked some switches and the screen came to life. It showed a massive lake surrounded by forest and hills. It looked absolutely beautiful.

'Our school is set in the area near this lake and forest. We have not taken pictures of the actual school, but you can imagine that it is fairly spectacular,' said the professor, again working his moustache.

Strange, thought Barry, no pictures of the actual school, but so what? It has to better than Moorlake.

The pictures then moved to young people running in the woods, building wooden bivouwacs, riding on zip wires between trees, paddling canoes, using rifles, skiing in beautiful mountains. It looked amazing and Barry's mouth fell open and stayed open as individual pupils, about eighteen years of age, spoke to the camera.

'Gianeco's is amazing,' one student said. 'If you are looking at the film about the school and it looks good, let me tell you, in real life, it is a million times better.'

'No, a trillion times better!' another happy face shouted.

These pupils looked so alive, so fit, their hair shone and their eyes just glowed with a sense of joy and fun. Barry could not help but compare these faces, these people and what they were saying, to the thugs at Moorlake. There was such a difference. The students clearly loved their school and what they did in lessons. If Gianeco Leapos was an exciting prospect before, now it was simply irresistible. Or was it?

After about five minutes of this mouthwatering show, the professor asked Russell to turn the machine off and, with his sparkling eyes fixed on Barry, he asked the question.

'OK then, Barry, are you with us, a St. Gianeco Leapos pupil, or are you going to Moorlake? Only you can choose.'

Barry looked at Nina and Russell, both smiled back. Two friends already made, he thought.

'I would love to come, Sir, it looks absolutely amazing and your pupils look so fit and happy. BUT, and you know this already, Sir, I can't come without Raza.'

The eyes of all the adults met. They had been expecting this, but thought that that the 'film show' might have weakened even Barry's determination not to be separated from Raza. Barry knew nothing of the special status that his DNA, fingerprints and iris test gave him and he knew that he was probably closing the door on a place at what seemed from the film to be the most stunning school in the world.

The Professor spoke first.

'I'm afraid that's not possible, Barry. We came here today with one place available and one only. The education that we provide is very expensive, we cannot just create another, extra place. We have enough money for twenty children every seven years and we can do nothing about it, I'm afraid.'

Barry looked at Nina and Russell again. He would have loved to have just smiled, changed his mind and accepted the place. After all, Raza was bright, he could cope on his own. But Barry knew that it was not to be, he would never let Raza down and he would just have to refuse this amazing offer, no matter what.

'I'm sorry, Sir,' he said. 'I would love to come, but you know that I cannot, without Raza.' As he spoke, his voice broke a little, letting everyone present know how much this was hurting him. A boy who had nothing, no home, no family was turning down a place at the most amazing school, because of his loyalty to a friend.

Barry stood and shook hands with the professor, who looked sad, and Russell who looked even sadder and then felt a massive lump in his throat grow as Nina took him in her arms and gave him a big hug and kissed his head. Barry, and children like Barry, are not used to being shown affection and he found it hard not to cry out loud.

With his eyes looking towards the floor, Barry left the bus and made his way back to the house. As he passed Raza on his way to the bus, he merely shook his head. Raza just mouthed, OK.

Raza entered the bus and sat at the same table that Barry had just left. He looked at Nina and Russell and the professor and felt their warmth. The film show was started and the professor began his sneaky little plan to test their loyalty and to split the boys if he could.

He thought that Raza would accept the place, which the professor would then withdraw, and offer it again to Barry, who by then would know that Raza had let him down and so would accept the place on offer. Not a nice plan, but it was important for the professor to get Barry to St. Gianeco Leapos Academy, and he would use whatever means he could to do it.

After the film show, Raza said in a very clear and confident voice. 'Thank you, professor, it looks an amazing place. I would love to live and study there.'

The adults looked at each other. The professor was confident that his plan was beginning to work. Nina and Russell just looked uncomfortable and awkward.

'But,' said Raza, 'without Barry, that will not happen. Thank you for a special day, I enjoyed your tests a lot!'

He stood up and began to shake the hands of the adults and left the bus!

The Professor was dumbfounded. He began to speak, but it was useless. Raza was going, there was no more to be said. After Raza had gone, the adults just sat in silence. The professor's plan had failed, the child they had been searching for, Barry, had declined a place at the academy and it seemed as if the whole day had been wasted.

Back in the Home, both boys sat on Barry's bed. Both were disappointed, but both were determined not to change their minds. They discussed the tests and what they had seen of the fantastic school. They both knew what they were giving up; a once-in-a-lifetime opportunity.

All of the adults on the 'Wonder Bus' began to pack equipment away and prepare for the journey back to the academy. They were all disappointed too. They had seen mental and physical records broken, special children recognised, and yet had nothing to show for all their hard work. The driver came into the bus and asked the professor if he was ready to leave.

'Give us a few minutes, Arthur, can you? We are just trying to sort a few things out. Russell and Nina, can you join me in the back.'

The professor and his two assistants went into the other part of the bus and sat down. The professor made a telephone call from the far end of the bus. Nina and Russell could not hear what was being said, but the professor had a strange look in his eyes when he returned. He spoke to them.

'Right then, you two don't think much of my plan to split up the boys, do you?'

Russell and Nina looked at each other, both embarrassed that their feelings had been so obvious. The professor was their 'boss', but they also respected him a great deal.

Russell broke the silence.

'Sir, it just seemed such a bad thing to do to ask the boys to be disloyal to each other. They are very special and their friendship is deep, it just seems wrong to play them off against each other.'

Nina nodded in agreement.

'So you think badly of me, Russell and Nina? I have behaved less than honourably?'

Russell and Nina just looked at the floor to avoid the searching, penetrating blue eyes of the professor.

'What if I told you it was the final test for them? What if I told you that the whole thing was designed to test their loyalty?

'What would you say if I told you that there is a place for both of them at St. Gianeco Leapos Academy?'

The professor had saved his brightest smile for this moment.

'You have known me long enough to know that I value loyalty and honesty above all other things. These two boys will be our star pupils, I am sure of this, and I am pleased that you feel the same way. You do feel the same way, don't you?'

Russell and Nina grinned from ear-to-ear and together they replied,

'Yes, yes, we do! But what about numbers? That makes twenty-one?'

'A rule, Russell, and rules have to be broken sometimes; at special times like these. The phone call has just confirmed it. This year we will have twenty-one pupils. There has always been one room that was never used at the school as you know, a spare room. We planned for a day like this some time ago, and today our plans have paid off. I have never seen two beginners, new students, with so much potential. Watching them develop and learn will be fascinating for us all.'

The professor stood and moved to rejoin the others in the back room of the bus.

'Well, we had better let these two boys know that we want them both, don't you agree?' asked the professor.

As the two boys made their way from the house to the 'Wonder Bus', they did not allow themselves to even consider the chance of a change of mind on behalf of the professor. They entered the bus and smiled at Russell and Nina, who for some reason looked much happier than when they had left them earlier in the day.

Barry and Raza were still uncertain just what was going on and why this second interview together was happening.

The professor spoke first.

'I have just made a phone call. We now have two places at St. Gianeco Leapos Academy. We can have twenty-one students this year for the first, and probably only time. We would like to offer a place to each of you.'

The boys looked at each other, they could not believe what had just been said and they could not speak, such was their emotion and shock at the news.

'Well, are you coming or not?' asked the professor jokingly, as if he was getting tired of waiting for their answer.

'Yes, yes,' they both blurted out, 'of course, of course, when do we come, what do we bring, how do we get there, what will we study first..?'

'Whoa, whoa! Hang on,' said Russell laughing. 'We will answer all your questions in good time, for now, we just to need to know that you will accept the offer.'

Raza put on his most formal voice, as if he were reading the news on television.

'Barry and I would like to formally accept the offer of places at the St. Gianeco Leapos Academy, for this coming September,' he said.

'Then you had better give me another hug,' said Nina, 'and we can get back to make all the arrangements for your journey to the school.'

'We will get all the information to you through Mr. Goodall, so just be patient for now and make the best of the rest of your time here, because soon Freeman's Children's Home, and your time here, will become a distant memory.'

The boys shook hands with Russell and the professor, hugged Nina and began to leave the bus with probably the biggest smiles on their faces that had ever been seen. As they reached the door of the bus, Raza turned and looked at the adults.

'One last question, please. Where does the name St. Gianeco Leapos come from, who was he?'

The adults looked at each other, their faces gave nothing away, but the question definitely had had some impact on them. They had not expected this question at this time. The professor reacted first, his voice clear and warm.

'Oh, good question, Raza, one that we are frequently asked. He was a saint in Greece in very early times and we used his name because he was the patron saint of orphans in that country. A good choice, don't you think?'

The answer tripped off the professor's tongue easily, a practised reply and perfectly reasonable, but both boys sensed a change in his voice, something about that answer was not quite as it seemed. For now, this did not bother the boys at all. They ran, skipped, jumped and shouted all the way to their room, where they bounced on their beds for a full hour. They just could not believe their luck!

Chapter 11

Preparing to Leave

The days following the interviews had gone very slowly. The school holidays had begun and life at the home was even more dull during these periods. School was not great, but at least it filled the time and got the children away from the likes of Mrs. Dukes and Useless Eustace. Since the events in the school playground, Useless had been pretty quiet. He obviously felt that what had happened to Barry had taught him a lesson and that his own superiority has been confirmed.

Everyone knew what had happened and it made Useless feel big. The other children in the Home knew that he would not hesitate to make their lives a misery if they got on the wrong side of him, so everyone acted as if he was something special, the one to respect and to fear. They were right, Useless was getting even bigger for his boots and even more confident in his capacity to be the boss. In short, Useless needed to be pulled down a peg or two; he needed to be taught a lesson. Barry and Raza were making plans for just such a lesson. The timing would have to be perfect. It would have to happen just before their departure for St. Gianeco Leapos Academy. If they left him any time to get his own back, he would, and it would not be fun for the boys, as he was bigger, stronger, nastier than them and very dangerous.

The boys were due to leave Freeman's Home on August the 31st, ready to start the new term at St. Gianeco Leapos Academy on September the 1st. By now, the news that the two boys were leaving was common knowledge and people were forever asking them why they had chosen to go and what it was like there. Barry and Raza had agreed to play it down and not to mention the things that they had seen in the 'Wonder Bus' or about the film clips they had seen of the school. The last thing they wanted or needed was for the other children in the Home to think that they were running away from them and a future at Moorlake Comprehensive. This was, after all, what the rest of the children had; this was their life and Barry and Raza were too bright and too sensitive to rubbish it or criticise it. They just felt glad inside to be going elsewhere, and especially an elsewhere which seemed genuinely different and exciting. So, they confined their discussions and excitement to the quiet and private times that they had together, usually at night just before lights out.

As far as possible, they stayed out of sight and reach of Useless, and planned their revenge just as secretly, as they thought about their future.

The plan had to have something within it that would ridicule Useless, allowing other children to see him for what he was; a big, brutal bully. It also needed to be perfectly timed so that **all** the other children in the Home shared the joke and had the opportunity to watch Useless squirm.

The day was set. There would be quite a send-off party for the two boys on the 30th of August, and it was certain that all the staff and children of the Home would be there to say goodbye. Using this day also left no time for Useless to come looking for them and get his own revenge on them.

No, Useless would just have to live with the fact that Barry and Raza were both too clever and too quick for him. He would spend the rest of his life hoping for the chance to get even, but knowing that he probably never would. It was a perfect plan as far as the timing was concerned, just what to do and how to do it was more difficult, and the two boys could think of little else as they sat in the garden one warm and sunny August day.

CHAPTER 12

The Plan for Revenge

There are many types of fear. Every person in the world has some thing, or many things, that they are frightened of.

Some people fear heights and get dizzy just standing on a bridge or a ladder. Some people fear being drowned and hate being near water. Almost everyone is fearful of pain from injury or violence, though some people hardly show any signs of this when they are hurt.

Useless Eustace, despite his many bad bits, was a tough kid. He had never been seen crying when he was hurt. One day, some years before, he had fallen from a window in the home, broken his leg, smashed his face and had lots of other very painful injuries. But he had never cried or made much fuss. No-one would have guessed just what he had suffered. So, trying to hurt Useless was not a good idea, it would just make him look even tougher and harder and that could help to build his reputation. Luckily for Raza and Barry, there was something which Useless was afraid of, in fact he was terrified of. Spiders! And because the home was so old and dusty, there were lots of spiders around to help them with their plan.

The thing they needed was a means to capture some and then their plan could really begin to take shape.

First they collected some jars from behind the kitchen, taking great care that Mrs. Dukes did not see them. They collected some boxes and cut out flat pieces to be used in capturing the spiders. Then, using bits of flat card and the jars, they started their hunt.

They lifted old bits of carpet, moved objects, shook curtains and looked in and under every piece of furniture in the house; all the dark and dim corners where cobwebs gave the clue that spiders may be lurking. When a spider was spotted, one of the boys would put a glass jar over it, then the other would gently slip a card under the jar, being careful not to make too big a gap for the trapped animal to escape. Then, once secured in the jar, a piece of paper with holes pierced in it was fastened around the top of the jar with a rubber band.

They searched in their dormitory and then moved on to bathrooms. Behind pipes was a very rich source of spiders and then they secretly searched in other rooms, because if anyone had spotted them the plan could be ruined. Finally, with six large and – if you don't like them – scary spiders safely in jars, they made their way back to their dormitory.

Just as they were making their way up the stairs, who should be coming down? Useless! The two boys panicked, quickly put the jars into the box they were carrying and flipped the lid shut.

'What have we here? My two great little mates, Baza and Raza!' said Useless sarcastically.

'I hear you are leaving us and you won't be coming to Moorlake to play with my friends again. What a pity! They so enjoyed meeting you two the other day and they have lots of other things they would like to show you. They will be very disappointed in you two, and so am I.'

For this last sentence, Useless put on his most ugly and threatening face.

'Yes, Useless, we have been chosen to go to a school where you need a brain to get in, not just a big mouth and tough mates.' This was Raza, and hatred burned in his eyes as he spoke.

'Ooooooh! Chosen, were you, for that place where the teachers can't even spell, if their notice is anything to go by? I should be careful what you wish for, Raza, not everyone is straightforwardly nasty like me. Some people look very pleasant and honest, but underneath they can be all sorts of nasty things,' said Useless.

'Sure, Useless, you should have seen the videos they showed us, then you would know just how fantastic this Academy is that we're going to,' said Barry.

'And that, Baza, says it all. You see some stupid advert, have a crazy interview with weird people in a weird bus. Then they show you some pictures and you two, who keep telling me that you are clever, say:

Yes, please, I will come with you to whereever you want me to go.' He said this in a mocking voice.

'Seems to me you have been fooled, little boys. You know there is still a market for slaves in some countries. The fact is, you two have agreed to go somewhere you know nothing about and with people you know even less about. Good luck, lads, and I hope you enjoy whatever they have in store for you!'

And with that, Useless carried on down the stairs. He then turned and asked,

'What's in the box, then?'

'It's none of your business, Useless, so just carry on and get lost,' said Barry.

'Struck a nerve have I, Baz? You beginning to see just how stupid you have been? At least at Moorlake you knew who and what you were mixing with.'

'Quite,' said Raza, 'dopes like you.'

Useless smiled, he knew that he had upset the two boys. It showed on their faces and in their eyes; they both had their doubts about what they were going to do. Useless was partly right, where were they going to and who were the people who ran this academy? Of course, the professor and his helpers all looked respectable and even nice, but Useless was right. They could just be good actors, and there had been one or two moments when the professor was not being completely honest, both boys knew this. For instance, when Raza had asked about the name, Gianeco Leapos, something about the look on all the adults' faces and the professor's answer was not right, not absolutely honest. Raza would look into this and soon.

A stroke of genius then hit Barry. He knew that this would be a good time to lay the bait to get Useless to come to their leaving party.

'And, Useless, as you are so keen to know, the stuff in this box is for our leaving party tomorrow night, which you are not invited to. See yer, Useless,' said Barry as both boys ran up the stairs leaving Useless to think about how he could get to this leaving party and, if he could, ruin it for them.

Useless decided he needed to talk to Mr. Goodall. He knew that he could talk Goodall into letting him go to the party, he would promise to behave himself! Be a good boy. 'Fat chance,' he thought. 'Leaving here, for you two, is not going to be as easy as that!'

CHAPTER 13

The Leaving Party

The boys had been given permission to decorate the main commonroom at the house on the day of their party, the 30th of August, their last day at Freeman's Children's Home. All their friends joined in, blowing up balloons, putting sparkling tinsel everywhere and, by the time they had finished, even this gloomy old room looked brighter and ready to have some fun. It was probably the case that before the house had become a children's home, this room had seen lots of parties and been a place of great joy. Today it was remembering its past and the atmosphere was one of excitement and anticipation.

Parties were very rare at the Home and though Useless' words were still on the minds of Raza and Barry, they were in fine spirits, laughing, joking with everyone and doing their best to make this last occasion at the Home one that everyone would remember, including Useless. The academy was in the future and, for now, that could wait. Today was about saying goodbye in a proper and enjoyable way. To help with this, Mr. Goodall had arranged for food to be sent up to the Home from the local shops to spare the children the nightmare of eating Mrs. Dukes' pasties, pies, sausage rolls and sandwiches, which all tasted like dung.

Instead there were boxes of crisps, small cakes, chocolate biscuits, chocolate bars, pork pies, sausages on sticks, lots of not very healthy, but tasty food. For other children this would have been quite a good bit of party food, but for these children, used to Mrs. Dukes' terrible food, it was a feast, like nothing they had seen since Christmas; and even that was not quite as good as what was on offer tonight.

The children mixed, chatted and played in the big old room downstairs and this room, normally so dull and dismal, took on new life for a while. The children ate, they talked and they ate, and some just sat silently and ate. Being deprived of decent food can result in children thinking about nothing else. When you are hungry, you can only think about food; nothing else matters. So tonight, first of all the food had to be eaten and, though there was plenty, still the children wanted to get as much as they could eat inside them before the night was finished.

Most of the children had put on their best clothes for the party. These were not anything that most children would consider smart or cool, but they were the best that these children had, and anything was better than turning up in school uniform. All the children had washed their hair and for once they all looked fairly healthy and happy. The fact that Barry and Raza were actually leaving did not seem to have registered with many of the children present. Barry and Raza talked with as many people as they could, saying how they would miss everybody and how they would stay in touch. Both of the boys knew that they would not miss the Home very much and, though they promised to stay in touch with their old friends, they both knew that it was unlikely to happen or continue for too long after they had left. It was far more likely that the boys would become completely absorbed by their life at St. Gianeco Leapos Academy. Both boys would miss Philip and Sam, their younger room-mates. Though these two were fairly quiet kids, they had become close to Barry and Raza and, because they were a couple of years younger, they sort of looked up to their older friends.

Occasionally Barry would find Sam just looking at him, and then look away quickly when Barry caught his eye. Philip seemed to be following Raza around, not too closely, but staying within hearing distance of what Raza was saying. It was clear that at least two younger boys were going to miss Barry and Raza.

Useless Eustace was not at the party, but Barry and Raza knew it was only a matter of time before he turned up. They wanted him to arrive, either just before or during the games, which were just about to start.

Mr. Goodall stood in the middle of the room and asked the children to be quiet.

'R-R-R-R-Right th-th-th-then,' he said,
    'we had better get on with s-s-s-some g-g-games before it's t-t-t-t-too late! What's first, Raza?'

Raza spoke with absolute confidence, smiling at everyone as if he was used to speaking to large groups of people in public.

He said, 'OK, everyone, first of all I want to you look at the cards I gave you a minute ago with a number on it. This game is known as reverse bingo. When I call out the number that you have, you sit down and you are out of the game. The last person standing will be the winner. Have you got that?'

'Raza, Raza, what's the prize for the winner?' asked Sam.

'A big surprise, Sam. All the prizes tonight are surprises that Barry, myself or Mr. Goodall have provided,' he put on his most exciting face and voice and said, 'and they are extremely valuable, as I am sure you would expect!'

All the children replied with an 'oooooooh' and laughed. They had a good idea of just what the prizes would be, and valuable was not the word that came to mind.

'OK, let's go then. Are you ready?'

'Yes, yes!' screamed the children.

'First number, seventeen.'

'Oh,' said a girl to Raza's left and she sat down.

'Thirteen,' said Raza and another child sat down.

This was repeated about thirty times until there were only two children left.

The other children began to chant their names, 'To-ny,

To-ny, To-ny,' some called.

Others called 'Bo-bby, Bo-bby, Bo-bby.'

'Quiet,' said Raza and, with great dramatic skill, he put the cards behind his back.

'Left hand or right hand?'

'Left, left, left!' screamed some. 'Right, right, right!' screamed others.

'OK, hands up for left,' shouted Raza and he counted. 'Right, hands up,' and he counted again.

'A dead heat,' said Raza, 'twenty-one each. That means it's up to you to choose, Mr. Goodall.'

Mr. Goodall smiled. He knew Raza had done this on purpose to make him stammer even more than usual, but he was prepared. He took a deep breath and waited and then blurted out without the slightest stammer,

'Right!'

All the children laughed, appreciating the joke on Mr. Goodall, and Raza brought the card from behind his back. The two children waited, tense but smiling, appreciating the moment of suspense.

'Eight!' shouted Raza. 'Oh no!' shouted

Tony. 'Yes, yes, yes!' screeched Bobby. 'What's my prize, what's my prize?'

Barry reached into a big box and pulled out a box of chocolates.

'Wow!' said all the children, who had been expecting something else, not a real prize at all. They were amazed and Bobby was stunned as she stared at the box with cellophane on it, unused and unopened. What a treat!

A proper prize changed the nature of the games from here on in. The children became very keen to win, and games of mastermind, charades, musical chairs were played with real competition. Children who were normally quiet and gentle became like wild animals in search of success and the prizes it brought. Everyone was having a great time. Even Mr. Goodall lost his stammer for a while! Such was the fun, that no-one noticed someone else had quietly entered the room. Only Raza and Barry noticed the arrival of Useless Eustace.

He sat at the back of the room and watched the pro-ceedings, thinking just how he could ruin the evening for his enemies, Barry and Raza. He had a plan.

The prizes were getting better and better as the night wore on. More expensive toys appeared, the odd book or music CD; real presents which must have cost Mr. Goodall a small fortune. Useless made up his mind, he would wait for the last game and win the final and probably best prize of the night. Useless was not stupid and, being older than most of the other children, he knew that he had a pretty good chance of his plan succeeding.

'Right,' shouted Barry. 'This is the final game of the night and the best prize awaits the winner!' 'Yes, yes, it's me! It's got to be me,' various children shouted.

'There are rules here which have to be obeyed. If you have already won a prize, put up your hand.' About twenty children held up their hands. 'Well, as you have already won once, it's only fair that the others get a chance, do you agree?'

'Yes,' said all the children yet to win a prize. 'No, boo, boo, boo!' shouted all those who had. 'Well, that's how it is going to be, isn't it, Mr. Goodall?'

'Y-y-y-yes, of course, that's what we agreed, Barry.'

'OK, then here is the game. Everyone who is playing stands on one leg. When you fall or lose balance and the other leg hits the floor, you lose. There is one more thing, you have to do this blindfolded. All those in the game come over here and have your blindfolds on and then we can start.'

A voice from the back of the room got everyone's attention. 'I'll have a go at this one, Baza, let me in here.' All the children parted to let Useless through. The smiles left their faces and you could see the fear felt whenever he was around.

Barry and Raza looked at each other and at Mr. Goodall. There was nothing for it, Useless would have to be allowed to play.

'The other part of this game,' Barry went on, 'is that the winner has to leave their blindfold on to receive the prize as it is such a special treat; a real one-off.'

'Yeh, wonder what it is? Bet it's a bike; no, a computer; no, a game console!' the children argued.

'You will have to wait and see, won't you?'

said Barry. 'Let's get started.'

The blindfolds were put on, the players stood in the middle of the room and then Mr. Goodall started the countdown. Barry and Raza shared a look, and down by his side Raza showed Barry a secret thumbs-up. Their plan was working to perfection.

Minutes passed, children wobbled and fell, the others cheered as one by one the number left in the game decreased.

Soon only Useless and two others were left standing. They wobbled, then balanced again. Eventually one girl staggered and put her second foot down. Just two left. Secretly, Barry and Raza wanted Useless to win. Of course, none of the other children did!

The tension was mounting, the children began to chant,

'Sam, Sam, Sam!' The room-mate of Barry and Raza was the only one preventing Useless from winning. Sam went to the left, Sam went to the right almost banging into Useless. Then he went off to the left again, gathering speed with each hop, until he hit a chair and fell over.

'Boo! Boo! Hiss! Hiss!' the children cried.

'I declare Mr. Eustace the winner,' said Mr. Goodall. 'And the final prize of the night will be awarded by Barry Spotter.' Useless began to remove his blindfold.

'No, no,' said Mr. Goodall, 'we all heard Barry's rules for the last prize. It must be awarded to a blindfolded winner, even I don't know just what the spectacular prize will be.'
He took Useless by the arm and led him to the prizegiving chair.
'Here, sit down and rest a while, standing on one leg must be very tiring,' said Mr. Goodall.
'It was easy, dead easy,' said Useless.
The children all looked at each other and held their noses. They could do this because Useless could not see them. They all shared the joke.

'Come on then, Spotter, give me my present,' called Useless in his most unpleasant way.
'Oh, it's coming, Useless. I'm just reaching into the box now,' said Barry, with a knowing look at Raza.
'Come on then, get on with it. Is it an iPod, a CD player or what?' asked Useless.

'No, not quite, Useless. Here, you have a feel first and have a guess if you like.' He handed Useless a cylinder-shaped object, wrapped in coloured paper. Barry's face was full of tension now, he did not know just how Useless would react.

'I have no idea, could be a jar of sweets, could be a jar of money. It does feel like a jar,' said Useless.

'Well done, Useless, it is a jar. But what is inside it, that's the point?' said Barry.

'I give up,' said Useless.

'OK, take off the blindfold and carefully unwrap the prize, Useless,' said Barry.

Slowly Useless removed the blindfold while all the children watched in absolute silence. He then began to remove the paper very slowly, as it was sticking in places.

As he stared down at the prize being revealed, Useless' face began to change, his eyes went huge and his bottom lip began to quiver. He went red, and then white, and he froze in the chair as if he had seen a ghost. He was completely and totally terrified of what he had seen in the jar.

Four of the largest house spiders you have ever seen in your life were in the jar, and Useless felt as if he would die with fear. He could not move to throw them away, and in any case, he might end up with one in his lap if he tried.

Suddenly the other children began to see just what had done this strange thing to Useless. The toughest, biggest bully in the home, was a gibbering wreck.

They all pointed and laughed, shouted various insults and even those who did not like spiders themselves could not help but join in.

'So,' said Raza, 'Mr. Tough isn't so tough, is he? Look at him, the rest of you; see him for what he is, a big bully who is scared of harmless spiders. Now when we have gone tomorrow, you will always know just what Useless is made of. So don't be scared of him any more and don't let him bully anybody.

'Now, Mr. Hard Man, I'm going to help one of these little creatures escape and crawl all over you, in your hair, down your trousers, all over. How about that, Useless? This is known as revenge for what you did to Barry that day at Moorlake. Do you remember that, Useless, do you?' Raza almost spat the last few words out.

'Sorry,' murmured Useless, his voice barely audible. 'Sorry, sorry, don't do nothin' else, Raza.' Useless was close to tears, he was literally scared stiff, unable to move; almost unable to breathe.

'Please take them away, please, please,' he screamed.

'OK, that's enough,' said a voice from behind. 'Let him go and get those spiders out of his hands, Raza.' It was Mr. Goodall.

'With respect, Mr. Goodall, stay out of this. You did nothing when Barry was beaten up and you do nothing when this scumbag, Useless, does all sorts nasty of things to everyone here. So stay out of this, he has had this coming for along time. It's time he suffered.' Raza was angry and his normally beautiful eyes were full of hatred.

He moved to get a spider out of the jar to torture Useless even more.

'Stop,' said another voice, 'no more, Raz, that's enough.'

'No, it isn't, he deserves a lot more than this after what he did to you and what he has done to most of us here,' said Raza.

'I know that, Raz, but look, if we do this to him we will be just as bad as him and everyone here will remember us for being cruel and vicious. Is that what you want to be remembered as, someone like Useless? Let him go, Raz, take the spiders out of his hands and let's finish this now, we have had our fun.'

Reluctantly, with Useless still motionless and white with fear, Raza took the jar of spiders from the older boy's hands. With one last bit of spite, he jabbed the jar at Useless, who screamed and tears came into his eyes.

The other children looked on in silence as Useless got shakily to his feet and began to leave the room. He looked sad and dejected, as if a poison had been taken out of him but in losing the poison he had become weak and lifeless.

Bit by bit, the other children broke up and said goodbye to Raza and Barry. The girls who were bravest gave each of them a kiss on their cheeks, whilst the boys shook hands in a kind of embarassed way, knowing it was the thing to do but feeling awkward about doing it.

As they packed things away and put rubbish into plastic rubbish bags, Mr. Goodall looked at Raza and then looked away, unable to keep his gaze. He was ashamed that a small boy could be so right about his own weaknesses and aware that what Raza had said was indeed the truth. Mr. Goodall made a decision that night. He would never let the children in his care be bullied or picked on ever again.

The party was over. The last bit of it with Useless had rather spoiled the night for some children for a while, until the prizewinners began to share the prizes in their dormitories!

Barry and Raza lay in bed discussing the night's events in whispers so as not to wake the two smaller boys in their room who were already fast asleep.

'You were too soft, Barry, you to have beat your enemies good and proper,' said Raza.

'I know what you think, Raz, but look at it this way. When you were torturing Useless...'

'Torturing him? Torturing him? I had not even begun,' said Raza.

'Well, OK, when you were scaring him, I realised just what Useless is. He is a very sad and lonely kid, like all of us. He has never had anyone to love him. All he knows is that he has to look after himself because no-one else will. So, he is in a battle with the world, with everyone. All he knows is how to survive. He doesn't have friends either, real friends who look out for each other, like we do. His mates just use him and encourage each other to be as bad as they can be.'

'That's no excuse, Baz, we are all like that here. Children *in care* is what they call us, but we are not all like Useless,' said Raza.

'Raza, here we are talking, sharing our ideas and friendship. Useless is lying in bed still scared that a spider might crawl on him, and desperate because he has shown weakness to the other children. He has no-one to talk to, no-one to reassure him–'

'And planning on how to get even with us!' interrupted Raza.

'Yes, probably Raz,' laughed Barry, 'but he won't be able to, because we are leaving here in the morning. A new start, a new life. No more of Useless and no more of Mrs. Dukes' rubbish food. Night, Raz, it's the biggest day of our lives tomorrow, we're off!'

'I had almost forgotten! Let's get to sleep. Night, Baz,' said Raza.

Then Barry spoke in a very soft voice.

'Raz, have you noticed anything different about me since we were chosen for St. Gianeco's?'

'Yes, I have, Baz, you are going soft on the likes of Useless!'

'No, Raz, it's not that. Have you noticed something about the way I look?'

'What's going on here, Barry? Do you want me to tell you that you are handsome all of a sudden?'

'That would be nice, Raz, but no, it's not good to lie to your mates,' said Barry with a chuckle.

'It's my nose, it's stopped running all the time, it's normal. I'm eleven years old and for the first time in my life I don't have snot everywhere. It's great!'

'I'm pleased for you, Barry, but it never bothered me anyway. What's a bit of snot between mates?' said Raza with a smile. And both boys knew that was the cue for sleep.

What Barry did not know was that his wisdom had made a real impression on Useless. Useless would not forget Barry's kindness and it would make a much greater impression on him than any beating could have done. Being tortured would have just made Useless even more mean and nasty, but because Barry had shown him some mercy, Useless would begin to change, to become less brutal and more generous to those around him. The changes would be slow, but each day would see Useless become a warmer and better kind of person.

CHAPTER 14

Leaving the Home

When Barry opened his eyes on Saturday the 31st of August, it seemed like any other day. Somewhere during the night in his sleep, the importance of the day had been lost to dreams. The view of Raza and the other two boys still asleep was just like any other day. He rubbed his eyes, yawned looked around, and then! It hit him like a bolt of lightning! Today was *the day*, the day that he had been looking forward to for weeks, the first day of a new and exciting life away from this place which had been his home for as long as he could remember.

Just to confirm his thoughts, he looked around for his bags that had already been packed. There they were. This was not a dream, this was it. Barry and his best mate were off! He threw the covers off his bed and screamed and shouted at the top of his voice. 'RAZA, RAZA! Get up, get moving, it's time to go!'

That was enough. The room soon became a hive of activity. Raza and Barry rushed to the bathroom, where they washed and brushed their teeth for the last time in this cold and dingy place. With real pleasure, they removed their toothbrushes from the cups and did not bother to look back.

Back in the dormitory, the two smaller boys were busy trying to help. They carried things to Barry and Raza as they needed them to put into their cases and bags. For these two, Sam and Philip, this was a strange time. Of course they were caught up in the excitement of the moment, but there was also a note of sadness in losing their two bigger friends, whom they held in great regard, almost like two big brothers. Sam, in particular, just stared at Barry as he moved about, getting ready. And tears welled up in his blue eyes.

Barry and Raza carried their bags down to the entrance hall, down the wide steps, and Sam and Philip helped.

Barry could hardly swallow any breakfast. Such was the mix of emotions he felt inside that it gave him butterflies in his stomach, which would not keep still. He tried a bit of toast and a drink of tea, but it was no use, food was not what he wanted at all. Raza, on the other hand, seemed to have no nerves. He calmly ate his cereal, buttered his toast and slurped his tea as if it was any other day; nothing out of the ordinary. As people spoke to him, wishing him luck, patting his back, he just smiled his brightest and most charming smile. He said that he would keep in touch with everyone and that he was sure that they would be allowed to come back and visit their old friends sometime. Of course, this would probably not happen as Raza was not the sort of person to look backwards. But it was the right thing to say at the time, he thought, and it kept the conversations light and not too full of sadness.

Barry was feeling awkward and strange. He could not keep still. The excitement and anticipation of the new life were just too much for him to bear sitting at a table. So, he excused himself and went outside to see if some fresh air would help him to calm down. It was a beautiful day. The air was fresh, the sun already warm and there was no wind. He could hear the noise of birds only, and for once, this place seemed peaceful and even nice. He walked across to the old bench and sat in silence. He looked out across the fields in front of him and he thought just how much his life had changed in the last few months. One badly written advertisement, one rotten day at Moorlake Comprehensive, a few strange tests and interviews with George Clifford and Russell and Nina, and his life had been changed completely. **What he did not know, was that his life was about to change more than he could ever have dreamed.** He then heard a voice. That voice. Oh no, thought Barry. Not now, Useless, not just when I am leaving. Please leave me in peace.

'Oy, Spotter, can I 'ave a word with you?'

'Sure, Useless, what you gonna do now, beat me up just before I go? Spit on my head, put dog dirt on my back?'

'No, Spotter, you've got the wrong idea, I'm not here to be like that.'

Barry looked at Useless and there was something different about him. He lacked the wildness in his eyes and he was not threatening or aggressive.

'Look, Spotter, I am grateful for what you did last night. I wouldn't have done it for you. I would have watched you squirm,' said Useless.

Barry started to speak, but Useless held up his hand and stopped him. This was hard enough for Useless and he did not want any interruptions.

'Look, Spotter, what I did to you at Moorlake was wrong. I am sorry for that. It's hard for me, everyone expects me to be hard and nasty. So I play the game, but I don't like it and I want to stop.

'You're alright, Spotter, and I 'ope it goes OK for you in this new place where they can't spell.' He said this with a faint smile on his face. Barry noticed what a pleasant smile it was, something he had never seen before.

Barry returned the smile and said, 'You did me a favour really, Useless. I might not have gone for an interview if I had not been roughed up at Moorlake. But I accept your apology.' Then something happened that Barry could never have predicted. Useless held out his hand to shake Barry's, and as he did so, he said, 'Good luck, Spotter.'

'Thanks, Useless,' said Barry shaking his hand back.

Useless turned to walk away towards the house and a late breakfast.

As he went, Barry shouted, 'Hey, Useless, do me a favour, will you?'

'Don't push your luck, Spotter. What is it?' replied Useless.

'Just look after little Sam and Philip a bit for me, they need someone to look out for them,' said Barry.

'I'll think about it, Spotter,' said Useless and carried on walking.

Barry sat and smiled a smile of real warmth. Who would have thought that would happen. Leaving this place on good terms with Useless! It was indeed a strange day. After a couple of minutes, Barry stood and sprinted back to the house. The car to collect him and Raza was coming at 10.30am. It was now just forty minutes before it was due to arrive.

CHAPTER 15

The Journey

As the time passed, Barry and Raza started to become anxious. They asked what time it was about every minute. It was now 10.45am and the car was fifteen minutes late. Some of the children who were waiting to wave the two boys off started to lose interest, and Barry and Raza began to consider some of the things Useless had said to them before the party. Just how much did they know about the people who were picking them up and taking them away? Was it all just an elaborate hoax, no-one would turn up and they would be left looking stupid, staying at the home and attending Moorlake, with all its dangers and threats?

But just as they were beginning to lose heart, they heard the sound of a car engine and its tyres on the drive. Barry and Raza shared a look of enormous relief. Then it appeared, a big shiny black car, a kind of mini-version of the '*Wonder Bus*'. As it pulled up outside the house, the other children stared. It was so clean and shiny, and written clearly along the side was 'St. Gianeco Leapos Academy'. The windows were made of dark glass which stopped people looking inside, keeping the identity of anyone in the back a secret.

After a few seconds, the front doors opened and out stepped an elderly gentleman. It was the same man that had driven the 'Wonder Bus', his name was Arthur. Then out of the other side of the car came a face that brought great joy to both boys. Nina, the lovely young woman who had been with the boys through the interviews and tests, had come along to take them back to the Academy. Her face was smiling as she looked at Barry and Raza.

'Sorry, we are a bit late,' she said. 'We got stuck in a bit of a traffic jam and then Arthur needed a little break on the way.'

She looked at Arthur, who smiled back and also made his apologies.

'Well, are you two ready?' she asked.

'Yes,' said the two boys simultaneously. The other children just watched as the two boys passed their cases and bags to Arthur, who put them in the boot of the car.

They too had been captivated by the presence of such a smart vehicle and the woman who held some kind of charm over almost everyone she met.

Finally, with a few hugs for Sam, Philip and Mr. Goodall, and lots of 'goodbyes', the two boys got into the back of the black car. They pushed the buttons to drop the windows and continued to wave to their old friends.

'Ready to go?' asked Nina.

'Yes please, Nina, let's go quickly. I can see Sam and Philip are trying not to cry. Let's go.'

Arthur started the engine and the car began to move off. All the children waved and shouted, 'Good luck!' 'Keep in touch,' said others. Barry and Raza waved back and smiled and laughed at the antics of their friends.

The car left the house behind and began to travel down the drive to the open road and away.

As they approached the end of the drive, both boys spotted a lone figure.

'Is that who I think it is?' asked Raza.

'Yes, it's Useless,' said Barry. 'Can you just slow down a bit please, Arthur?' asked Barry. 'Run him over if you like,' said Raza in a low voice, so Arthur and Nina would not hear him.

As Arthur slowed the car down, Barry lowered his window again.

'See yer then, Useless,' said Barry.

'Not if I see you first,' said Useless, again with that smile that Barry had never seen before today.

And with that the farewell was over. Useless, with his head down, made his way back up the drive and the car and its valuable cargo sped away on a journey of several hours to a new home, a new school and a new life for the two friends.

For the first half hour or so neither of the passengers in the car spoke. The silence was respected by the adults in the car, who knew that Barry and Raza just needed some time to think and reflect on the day so far, the night before, and to allow Freeman's Children's Home become part of the past, rather than the present.

It was Raza who broke the silence with a question for Nina.

'Does everyone arrive today?'

'Yes, Raza. We pick everyone up today, the 31st of August, ready to start the new term on the first day of September,' she said.

'So, how come you are with us, Nina, and not back at the academy waiting for the other pupils to arrive?'

'Oh, someone had to come with Arthur and I guess I drew the short straw, Raza.' She said this with a little laugh and turned to face the boys so that they could see her face.

'Actually I wanted to meet you two again. You did so well in the tests, Barry on the physical tests and you on the mental, or as we call them cognitive, tests that I thought it might be interesting to meet before you get settled in at the Academy. And I thought you would have loads of questions, but obviously I'm wrong!' Again this was said with a little laugh and the boys knew that she was teasing them a bit.

'Oh, we've got questions!' said Raza. 'Loads of them.'

'Well, come on, fire away, that's what I'm here for,' said Nina.

'OK, how long until we get there?' asked Raza.

'About four-and-a-half hours from now, is that right, Arthur?'

'All being well,' said Arthur, 'as long as we don't meet any more traffic jams.'

'Do we have any food for the trip?' asked Barry.

This made Nina smile.

'Of course we have, and loads of it. Too nervous for breakfast, Barry?' asked Nina. This woman certainly knew about children, she knew that Barry would have been too nervous to eat!

'How did you guess?' asked Barry.

'Oh, it's happened before, Barry, believe me you are not the only one whose stomach has been full of butterflies this morning. We'll wait until we are out in the country before we stop and have a little picnic, if you can wait that long, Barry.'

'Yes, of course, that would be great on a lovely day like today. A picnic, wow!' And he dug his elbow into Raza's side and laughed.

Raza smiled his contented, knowing smile. Today was going well.

'More questions,' said Nina.

Both boys fired questions at Nina, hardly allowing her time to draw breath.

What were the other children like?

What would be their first lesson?

How many people in a dormitory? They were amazed to hear that there were no dormitories. Each child had their own room and their own bathroom.

'Is this a school or a hotel?' asked Raza.

'It's a very special school, Raza, and you will love it,' said Nina.

For the next hour or so the journey sped away, and as the towns became less frequent the countryside took over. Arthur chose a spot to stop for the picnic. It was a lovely place with a small river which had large boulders to walk on. As soon as the car stopped, Barry and Raza made for the river and began to scramble up and down the rocks. Listening to the rush and gush of water, they spotted massive dragonflies as they darted over the rocks and water.

Arthur and Nina took a basket from the car and laid a rug on the grass. The boys came back from the river and looked at the pies and sandwiches that were in the basket. Two good meals in two days was a real treat and one both the boys did justice to. When they could eat or drink no more, the four of them began to help pack the remains and cups away. It was then, in this almost perfect moment, that the atmosphere changed. Suddenly Nina began to look serious and concerned. She looked up to the sky and asked the boys to be quiet for a while. Then they all heard it, a helicopter overhead. It was fairly low and seemed to be looking for something. It was plain black with no police or ambulance markings on it.

'Quick!' said Nina. 'Get packed as quickly as you can and let's get moving.'

'What's wrong?' asked Barry.

'Nothing serious, Barry, but we have to keep an eye out for these helicopters sometimes, and I have to report the sighting to the school straight away.' Nina went away from the others, opened up her mobile phone and made what seemed a fairly important call. Judging by her face, the helicopter was not good news.

By the time she got back to the car, everything was ready and Arthur was behind the steering wheel ready to go.

Nina seemed to be back to her normal happy self and whatever had upset her was forgotten for the time being. Still Barry and Raza shared a few worried glances. They both thought the same thing. Just as everything seemed fine about the Academy, something a little strange had happened, which did not have a logical explanation and did not seem to fit with their ideas about the place and the people they had met. Firstly, when Raza had asked the Professor about the name of the academy, his answer had seemed somehow suspicious and then again, just now, something about the helicopter had definitely upset Nina for no apparent reason.

'OK, Arthur, next stop St. Gianeco Leapos Academy!' said Nina.

'Yes!' shouted the boys from the back and the journey continued through amazing countryside with hills and valleys and rivers and forests.

They hardly passed any other vehicles or people. So wherever this school was, it was very remote and a long way from any major city or town. Soon the main road gave way to a much smaller road and then eventually a forest track. There were no signposts and nothing to tell anyone where they were. Again the words of Useless entered Barry's head,

'*You meet some strange people who can't spell, do some stupid tests and then just go away with them. There is still slavery you know, countries where children are bought and sold!*'

The forest became deeper and darker and the paths went in all directions. It would be an easy place to get lost and very hard to find anything or anyone. Arthur drove the car with great confidence, turning right here and then left and then right again. Raza had looked at his watch when they entered the forest. They had been travelling through the forest for over an hour. Nina must have guessed that the boys were beginning to wonder where they were going and when, if ever, they would reach this remote and secret school.

'OK, Barry and Raza, we are nearly there. As you can see, our academy is in a very secret place. As we go around this next bend, I want you both to close your eyes and then when I say, and not before, open them for your first view of St. Gianeco Leapos Academy; your new school and your new home.

'OK, close those eyes,' she said.

The boys closed them tight. 'Now open them!'
    The boys were struck dumb.
    In front of them was a break in the forest, but all they could see was a massive lake or reservoir with a road leading down to some huge gates which appeared to lead under the lake.
    Arthur stopped the car. There was silence.
    Raza was the first to break the silence.

'OK, so where is the school? I can see the swimming pool, where are the classrooms?' he said.

'Just take your time, boys, have a good look at this and tell me what you notice. It's your first test!' said Nina.
    The boys stared and stared. Then it hit Barry first.

'There are no waves or any movement on the surface of the water, no birds, nothing,' he said.

'Well done, Barry. What looks like a lake is, in fact, the roof to our underground school and a roof that lets in so much light that it always seems like a sunny day in the school. But being underground makes it easy to heat and avoids the high winds and loads of other benefits that you will learn about during your time here. What do think?' she asked.

'Weird,' the boys said simultaneously.
  'Really weird!'
  Their mouths were still open as Arthur started the car again and began to move down the steep drive towards the front of the underground school. At the bottom, Arthur stopped the car.

'Shall I take the bags for Barry and Raza, Nina?' he asked.
  'What do you think, boys? Independence or being waited on, it's your choice?'
  'We'll carry our own bags, Nina. Thanks for bringing us here, Arthur,' said Barry.

Raza looked at Barry as if he was a little stupid for not taking the opportunity to have their bags carried for them, but decided not to try and argue. Instead, he thanked Arthur too, who was smiling at the good manners shown by the boys and impressed by the choice they had made.

These two will be OK, he thought to himself. Yes, these two are a bit special!
  'Thank you, Raza and Barry, I've enjoyed the journey. I have high hopes for you two. I know you are going to love your time with us here,' said Arthur.
  Nina and the boys got out of the car and the boys struggled to the glass doors with their bags. The car moved off to the right where what looked like huge garages had been dug out from under the ground.

The front of the underground school was all glass. Large windows formed the front of school which was shaped like a half-circle. In the middle were large doors that led to the huge entrance hall. The boys struggled with their bags through the doors and into the entrance hall.

The hall was filled with light, and had a wonderful sense of almost being outside in the fresh air. What made the entrance more impressive were the pictures on the walls. There were huge paintings side by side with huge action pictures of past pupils doing all sorts of outdoor activities, such as skiing, climbing, canoeing and walking over rope bridges. Barry thought that he recognised one of the pupils in the picture from the short film they had watched during the interview.

The most amazing thing of all, and it took the boys' breath away, was hanging from the ceiling by steel cables and wires. Hanging there, above them, was a real life aeroplane. And not just any old plane, but an actual fighter plane from the Second World War.

Raza spoke first, 'That's a Spitfire, a real Spitfire from the Second World War.'

The boys looked at the plane with a sense of disbelief. The plane had been left with evidence of its service in the skies. It still had bullet marks on its fuselage and dents in the wings. These scratches and dents just made the plane even more impressive. Nina allowed the boys time to take this all in. It was always the same with new pupils; they were always stunned by the first impressions of the underground school. What was even more stunning for Barry and Raza was that this school was almost the complete opposite of Freeman's Children's Home, where it was dull and often dark, even in the middle of the day.

This place was ablaze with light, and somehow, it just seemed full of life and activity and action.

'Well spotted, Raza, it is, and at the other end of the school we have another fighter plane from the war, a Hurricane. You will see that tomorrow when you have a guided tour of the whole school.

'But first we have some people to meet. Come this way!'

Behind the Spitfire was another wall of glass which formed the end of the entrance hall. Beyond this, the space was taken up with a long bright corridor with rooms on either side. Barry and Raza stared at what they saw through the windows of the classrooms as they walked down the corridor. There were science rooms with gas taps and fume cupboards, rooms full of headphones, computers, individual cubicles, like the one that they had used during the interview on the '*Wonder Bus*'.

There were rooms with gymnasium equipment and others with just rubber mats on the floor. As they made their way down the corridor, they spotted an office at the far end.

The boys ran a bit to catch up with Nina, their mouths still open and eyes staring at all that was around them, then went through the door and down another corridor, again decorated with paintings and pictures.

At the bottom of this second corridor was a door and, as the boys got closer to it, they read the name plate.

In gold letters it read:

PROFESSOR GEORGE CLIFFORD PH.D. PRINCIPAL

Nina knocked quietly on the door and a cheerful voice, which the boys recognised, called, 'Enter!'

'Well hello, you two, we have been waiting all day for this. You are the last to arrive,' said the professor. He turned to Nina with a more serious look.

'I hear you had some problems with traffic, Nina, but all is well now I hope. The whole year group has arrived safe and sound, ready for a new term and a new year. I always find this time so exciting.'

He said this with a real sense of pleasure and fun. Though the professor had seen many groups of children come and go, he did indeed find a new group very exciting and this particular year group had at least two very special and unusual members. He was looking forward to seeing just how Barry and Raza would get on.

What the professor knew, and at this stage Barry did not know, was that Barry's parents had been very special people, very gifted athletes who were extremely good at their jobs. Though Barry knew nothing of his parents, who they were or what they had been, Professor Clifford certainly did and one day he would share this knowledge with Barry. But not yet. He would wait for the right time.

As for Raza, the professor had not yet managed to find out anything about the boy's past or his original family. This, the professor found very interesting and he had ordered several people to carry on searching for information on this second outstanding young boy, who had unique mental powers.

'Barry, Raza, come, come in!' he said.

And both Barry and Raza saw that the old man was genuinely pleased to see them again. The sparkle in his eyes was even brighter today than it had been on the day of the interview. He shook both their hands and asked them to sit down. This they did as Nina watched, standing by a window with a smile on her face, watching her 'boss' work his magic on these two boys, of whom she was already very fond.

It never ceased to amaze Nina just how skilled the professor was at making children and young people feel comfortable in strange surroundings; how he used his charm to make them feel important and valued. He was a master. And the ability came from a genuine love of children. He **did** find them interesting and he **did** enjoy their company and he liked to laugh with them and marvel at their brilliance when they were given a chance to flourish. Every child he had ever met had something within them that could be developed into something special. Some were just outstandingly clever, like Raza, but others had qualities, such as courage and bravery. The list was endless.

The trick, the professor knew, was finding exactly what interested and excited them and then to develop this interest to its full potential. That was what Gianeco Leapos Academy was about. Well, it was mostly about this, but the school did have one or two other purposes, which the boys would discover later!

'Right then, Barry and Raza. Today, or what is left of it, we will show you to your rooms, then we will all meet for dinner, or evening meal, if you prefer to call it that. I shall give my little welcoming speech and then you will meet the other pupils for a while. Then you will try and get some sleep before our first real day of term tomorrow.

'Nina, will you take Barry and Raza to their rooms now and I will prepare my speech!' Nina laughed at this. She knew that the professor would make exactly the same speech as he had made many times before. She knew all his old jokes, almost the whole speech, word for word.

'Let's go and see if they have a room for each of you,' said Nina.

The professor held open the door and the two boys and Nina left the professor's room. Instead of going back down the corridor to the main entrance hall, they turned right and went down a shorter corridor to a circular area with doors going almost all round the whole of the circumference. All of the doors opened onto the circular area. Nina stopped in the middle of the round wooden floor.

'This circle is our *"meeting circle"*. Whenever you are asked to gather together, this is where you will come. Often at the end of the day or in the morning, we will all meet here so that you can be given information and instructions. Those doors on the far side are the rooms for the pupils, one each. As you two were the last to be selected this year, you are in rooms 20 and 21, next door to each other. We thought that would please you. So, would you like to see your rooms?' she asked.

Both boys nodded and made their way over to the crescent of doors facing them.

Rooms 20 and 21 were on the far right hand side of the crescent. Outside the doors both boys stopped and looked at each other.

'It was your original idea, Baz, you can have the first. Yours is 20 and I will have 21,' said Raza.

'Perfect,' said Nina. Both boys looked at each other again, wondering why the choice was perfect. When they opened the doors, they saw why Nina had made the comment. Inside number 20 was a huge sign which read,

'WELCOME BARRY'

and in number 21 another saying,

'WELCOME RAZA'.

Nina and the professor had guessed right. They had predicted what would happen from what they knew of the two boys.

Just like the other places in the school, the boys' rooms were full of light, but more, much more than this. Each of the rooms had a bed, dressing tables, wardrobes, all the usual things that bedrooms have. But these were made of a light wood and everything matched. The light entered the room through a window in the ceiling, which looked out on to the sky and the top parts of trees. In a part of the room was a desk and on it was a laptop computer and what looked like a games consul. There was also a wind-up radio and wind-up torch.

There was a picture on the wall in each of the rooms, a large picture of each of the boys taken in the same style as those of past students in the main entrance of the school. The only difference was that the picture in room twenty was of Barry doing his physical test during his interview in the '*Wonder Bus*' and in room twenty-one was one of Raza, working on the mental tests in the kiosk on the bus.

The pictures were very big, covering a large part of the wall. Both boys in their separate rooms just stood and looked at each of their images in the frames. Both thought exactly the same thing.

I belong here. I can be like one of those people in the film, like those on the pictures in the entrance hall. I am going to love this school.

At the back of each of their rooms was another door, and this led to a small bathroom. In each bathroom there was a sink, toilet, shower and small bath. There was soap and toothpaste already there and a range of things from nail clippers to hair brushes.

After a while, Barry left his room and went next door into room 21. Raza was sitting on his bed. He looked happy.

'Well, what do you reckon?' asked Barry.
'Nice picture,' he said with a laugh.

'Have you got one?' asked Raza.
'Course, and it's better looking than yours, ugly mug,' said Barry as he grabbed Raza around the neck and wrestled him into a lying position.

'Give up, loser, or you are dead,' said Barry.
'Never,' said Raza. 'You will soon see who is a loser!' And the two boys fell off the bed and onto the floor, both

shouting for the other to give up as they wrestled. Nina came into the room.

'Truce!' she cried. 'It's a draw.'

'I had him all the time,' lied Barry.

'You have been saved by Nina, my friend,' said Raza. 'I was just about to deliver my killer blow.' And he swung his arm in a karate chop motion.

'Are you impressed with your rooms?' asked Nina.

'Bit small, don't you think, Raz?' said Barry with his most snooty look.

'Yes, and I don't think my picture shows me at my best,' joked Raza.

'Oh well, we will see what we can do to put things right for you. I'm sure such honoured pupils deserve only the best,' said Nina, enjoying the boys' humour.

'But for now, the rooms will do?' she asked.

'For now,' said Barry. 'They are fantastic, this whole place is fantastic, better than I could have imagined. I can't wait to get started on the lessons.'

'Me too,' said Raza.

'All in good time,' said Nina, 'but first you had better unpack your things and then you can meet the other students before we all eat our first meal together. Tonight all the teachers have to attend and as many other staff as possible, so that the new pupils can get a look at all of us. So if you two get moving, we will all meet in the circle outside your rooms at about six o'clock. See you there,' said Nina and waved a goodbye.

'Barry, I will come to your room just before six o'clock so that we can go out together, is that OK?' asked Raza.

'Good idea, Raz, it's a bit scary meeting all these new people in one go. See you in about half an hour then,' said Barry, and he left to go back to his own room.

For the first time in his life he had a space to call his own and what a room it was! It had everything he needed, and his best friend in the world was just next door. Life was looking good and Barry was beginning to lose any doubts he may have had about coming to this school.

Chapter 16

Introductions!

At exactly ten to six, Raza knocked on Barry's door. The door opened immediately as Barry had been waiting nervously for his friend to arrive.

'Come in, Raz, how are you feeling?'

'Nervous, Barry, to be honest, but excited as well,' said Raza.

The two boys heard doors opening and closing, and the low chatter of voices outside Barry's room. They looked at each other and Raza checked his watch. It was time to go, but both boys were anxious. The last time they had experienced anything like this was at Moorlake Comprehensive, and that was not a good memory for either of them. The other thing that added to their anxiety was that meeting people for the first time is always a bit scary, but when you are only eleven years old in a brand new place and are not really sure what is expected of you, it's terrifying!

'Come on, Baz, at least we know each other, no-one else has come with anyone they know, that's what the professor told us,' said Raza.

'You are right, Raz, let's go!'

Both boys left Barry's room to see the meeting circle quite full with a mix of other children and adults.

The boys looked for a friendly face and saw Nina, who smiled and beckoned them over to her side.

'I hope this is not becoming a habit with you two; the last to be selected, the last to arrive and the last to join the circle!' she said with a smile.

'We-we-we-' Barry began to stammer.

'I'm only joking, Barry, you are not late. We are a bit early,' she laughed. 'Look, there's Russell, he is dying to see you two again.' She caught Russell's eye and pointed at Raza and Barry.

As Russell began to make his way over to the two boys, it gave them a chance to look around. The number of girls and boys looked about even. What struck Barry was that although the children were all supposed to be about eleven years old, they differed in size quite a lot. Raza was one of the smallest, some of the girls in particular were very tall and looked a bit older than the boys in general. He also noticed that there were a range of types and races of people in the group of children. The one thing that all the children shared was that they all looked nervous. As they looked around, very few spoke and if they caught the eye of another child looking at them, they would quickly look away. This happened to Barry a number of times. Then, as he looked away, he immediately caught the eye of a black boy in a yellow shirt looking at him. This time the boy did not look away, instead he smiled, his eyes lit up and his teeth gleamed in a friendly way. Barry could not help it, he smiled back immediately. It felt good, he almost felt as if he had made one friend already.

Then, as he turned his head, he was still smiling as he looked at a small girl who had lovely shaped eyes which Barry associated with Chinese people. When she saw Barry smiling, immediately her face lit up and she beamed a smile back at him. Barry decided to stop smiling. While it was good to 'make friends' in this way, he did want people to thing he was a lunatic with a permanent smile on his face! Raza gave him a quizzical look. He had remained calm and confident-looking during this time. Raza was a good actor!

Then Russell shook the hands of both boys and fired questions at them about their journey, their room and their last days at Freeman's.

Before the boys could answer all his questions, a loud 'gong' was heard and this was a signal for Russell to speak to the whole group.

'Welcome everyone. The gong is the sign that our food is ready and you are about to experience your first meal here at St. Gianeco Leapos Academy. I hope you enjoy it. Please follow me to the dining room.'

Russell then left the meeting circle and led the whole group of adults and children down a corridor to another room which contained six round tables, with six chairs around each of them. To the left of this, all down the side of the room, was a serving hatch that had very bright lights in its ceiling. Behind this was an enormous kitchen area with about six people, all busy preparing or carrying food from the cookers and ovens to the serving hatch.

Unlike at Freeman's Children's Home, the kitchen area looked spotlessly clean and modern. All the chefs were dressed in clean, striped trousers and white chef coats without collars; they all wore tall hats, which made them look very impressive.

As the children and adults walked into the dining room, Russell and Nina took control and asked the children to fill the tables in turn.

Barry and Raza managed to get on the same table and sit down.

When everyone was seated, Russell spoke again.

'Well done all of you, that's the first bit done! I know all of you are nervous and at the moment this all feels strange. A new school, new home, new people all around you, but soon this will be a real home to you and all these rooms and halls and corridors will be as familiar as the places you have just left. Before we eat tonight, I need to introduce you to our chief chef, Senior Luigi.'

He then raised his arm to point at a man behind the service counter. Luigi had a dark moustache and a small beard on the point of his chin. He had a huge smile on his face and his thick muscular arms stuck out of the end of his chef's coat. He walked to the far end of the service hatch.

'Shall I begeen, Mr.Russelli,' he asked.

'Please, Luigi, we can hardly wait,' replied Russell.

Luigi began, 'Ho-K. Letta me see what we 'ave fora you tonight. 'Ere we 'ave a the meats. We 'ave beef, chicken and a little bit of turkey.

'Then we 'ave the vegetables and the pasta. There is lots for you to try. I 'ave cooked them especially for you.

Then we 'ave a salad, lettuce, peppers, tomatoes and lots more!'

Luigi smiled and looked all around the room, catching the eyes of every child there.

'EEt is a my job to keep you well fed and 'appy. BUT, I do not want a lot of a fatties here at Gianeco, so I always cooka the gooda food, 'ealthy food. Some-a days we let you come into our a kitchen and a cooka for your friends. Thees is a reala treat and when you leave this school, you will all know just how to cooka beautiful food!'

He said this with his finger and thumb making a circle, held up next to his mouth.

'My 'elpers 'ere are very gooda chefs too and they will sometimes cooka speciala meals from all arounda the world. Tonight, try whata you want, but dona maka your selfa sicka! Enjoy!'

He spoke with such passion about his food, Raza and Barry could not help but compare this warm, enthusiastic man with the awful Mrs. Dukes, and the difference could not have been greater. The food was also very different. Everything was beautifully cooked and presented. Everything was fresh and full of flavour. The only problem was choosing just what to eat when there was so much to choose from!

After several visits to the serving area, both boys – and all the other children – began to feel full and unable to eat or drink anything else. It was interesting to see just how the conversation began to develop as the children lost some of their fear and shyness. Barry began to talk to the black boy with the lovely smile as they chose bits of turkey for their plates. His name was Émile and he was as friendly as his smile had suggested he would be.

As the plates were emptied and everyone looked fed and contented, Professor George Clifford entered the dining area. Without a word being spoken, the room became silent and the people working in the kitchen stopped what they were doing and sat quietly.

All eyes went to the professor.

'Good evening to you all,' he said to the people sitting at the tables. Then he turned his eyes to the serving hatch.

'Are they all fed, Luigi?' the professor asked.

'Si, Senor, they 'ave eat-a me of a 'ouse and 'ome, as you say in Eengland!'

'Good, then I will have a captive audience, I hope,' said the professor. He continued,

'You are all very welcome here. You are lucky to be here, you have been chosen from the many children who responded to our advertisement and those who were chosen for an interview.'

He spoke slowly.

'<u>BUT</u>, we are lucky to have you too. You have been chosen because you are all very special young people. St. Gianeco Leapos Academy is a special place too, you know this already from what you have seen. But it is far more special than you can yet know and, over the coming weeks and months and years, you will see just how extraordinary it is.'

The children and adults were all captivated by this small, but somehow, very impressive man. His moustache was twisted to perfect points. His suit and waistcoat were immaculate. His shoes shone like glass. He continued, looking at each child as he spoke.

'We do not have separate *houses* here, like in other schools. We do not believe that you should compete with each other all the time. We are one family at St. Gianeco's and we work together, not against each other. The only person you need to compete with here is yourself. What we want is for you to become the best that **YOU** can be, at whatever you choose to do. We will expect you to be disciplined, dedicated, courageous, honest and generous to each other. We expect you to obey the rules that we have here to keep you safe and to allow us to do our job. There are only twenty-one of you and, if all goes well, there will be twenty-one of you in seven years' time.

Twenty-one individuals, twenty-one independent young people full of knowledge and skills to help you to make your way in the world. For now, just what that way will be, is not important.'

The professor gave the children a moment or two to take in what he was saying.

'You will follow a very different curriculum from normal schools. You will learn karate, jujitsu, and other forms of self-defence. All of our students become black belts in at least one martial art, some become black belts in several.

All of our students will speak at least three foreign languages, some will learn several more.'

At this point he looked at Raza, knowing exactly what Raza was thinking. Raza would love to learn

Arabic, Chinese and Russian if he could. And if he could, he would!

The professor continued to talk to the spellbound audience in front of him.

'You will learn to ski, to mountain climb, to canoe and all of you will learn to fly a glider and some of you may progress to flying engined planes. Not our Spitfire though, or the Hurricane, they are out of bounds to all of us!

'We already know a lot about each of you and we will learn more. You will learn lots about yourself and you will develop skills that you never dreamed you would have.'

Again the professor paused and then pointed to the pictures of past students hanging around the room.

'These pictures of our past students will soon become history, to be replaced by pictures of each of you skiing, climbing, canoeing, running, doing a million-and-one things that we will make possible for you. Some of you may have been wondering why our poster that we put up in your homes and schools was written and spelt so badly. Well, you have all met me and Nina and Russell and Arthur, do we strike you as stupid people?'

He paused here and looked at the adults he had just mentioned. They were not stupid.

'No, we are not stupid. Our notice was designed to attract those children, like each of you, who do not fear the unusual, those who are not bound by conventions and the normal rules. We have a broad view of what is clever too. We know that some people, who cannot spell or read well, are extremely intelligent in other ways. We know that each of you has within you, special talents, it is our job to find these talents and to develop them.'

The professor paused to allow his words to sink in.

'You are now part of the St. Gianeco Leapos family. You are welcome. You are valued. You are special and you will make us proud of you during your time here, I am confident of this.' The professor smiled as he looked around the room.

'Yes, you will make us proud of you. Now I think you all need to get a good night's sleep, because tomorrow you have a big day ahead. It is the first day of your new life. You will discover that you need lots of sleep and energy here. It's fun, but it's hard work too! Are there any questions?'

The girl with lovely eyes, who Barry had smiled at, held up her hand.

'Sir,' she said. 'Do we have a school uniform?'

'Good question, Gemma,' said the professor, he already knew all the children's names.

'No, we do not. We want to develop individuals here, not people who are all the same, and a school uniform does not really fit with that aim. When you get up tomorrow you will find several catalogues of clothing will be given to you. We give you each an amount of two hundred pounds to spend on clothing, to add to what you already have. You can order this from the catalogues. This is the start of your independence! Specialist clothing for bad weather, martial arts and other special activities, like rock climbing, we will provide for you. The two hundred pounds is for you to choose the clothes that you want to wear at other times.'

The children looked at each other and it was clear that this was an unexpected, but welcome, treat.

'Are there any other questions?' the professor asked.

There were none.

'Well, we will all meet tomorrow for breakfast and then we will set about getting to know each other even better. Good night and sleep well, all of you.'

The professor gave a quick nod of the head to Russell and Nina, then quietly left the dining room.

The room was quiet. Of course the children had lots more questions, but for now they had more than enough to take in and the professor was right, they were tired. They needed sleep. Children began to stand and make their way to their rooms. As Barry reached number 20, he looked to his right and there was Raza. Both boys shared a smile and a nod. It was very clear. Both of them could hardly believe their luck.

CHAPTER 17

The First Day

None of the new pupils – and they were all new – had thought about how they would wake up, or what time breakfast would be ready. They had no need to worry. At seven o'clock all of the televisions in all of the rooms came to life. Some soft music, which gradually became louder, was played and on the screen was the message:

> *'Good morning. Welcome to your first real day at St. Gianeco Leapos Academy. Breakfast will be served in the dining room from 7.30am. Your tour of the school will begin at 8.30am.'*

Barry was already awake when the music began. He looked at the screen and he thought just how different this place was to the Freeman's Home. He got up, went to his bathroom and started to get ready for the day ahead. He was excited and a little nervous. His friend had woken at 6am, was dressed and out of his room by 6.30am. Raza did not like to sleep too long. His mind and imagination were too active for too much sleep!

Raza had walked all around the school by himself and he had noticed the different styles of classroom. He had stared at the other hanging plane, the Hurricane. He had stood and noticed all the bullet marks on the fuselage, and marvelled at the shape and the propeller, the wings where the guns had once been loaded to help to shoot down enemy planes. Raza knew that he would love to fly a plane one day and he hoped that what the professor had said about them learning to fly would start as soon as possible.

He walked the corridors in silence, and when he came close to the professor's office, he heard voices. He recognised them immediately. He heard Nina, Russell and the professor in deep conversation. Of course he knew it was wrong to listen to other people's conversations, but his curiosity got the better of him and he stopped and listened.

'Where exactly were you when the helicopter came over, Nina?' asked the professor.

'About an hour or hour-and-a-half from the school, sir,' she replied.

The professor continued, 'They are getting closer to us all the time, I do not think we will be able to use this place for much longer. In my opinion, this group that are just starting will be the last that we train here at St. Gianeco. We will need to be especially vigilant and careful over the coming weeks and months. This group look, to me, to be the most promising lot that we have had for years. The Spotter boy, we know, has the parents and genes to be exceptional. Several others would seem to have all the qualities we look for in our most able and promising pupils.'

'I think we need to let the pupils know the emergency rules as soon as possible, to avoid any problems if the helicopters come over again,' said Russell.

Raza listened to all this and his razor-sharp mind was already trying to make sense of the conversation.

How would these people know anything about Barry's parents? He was supposed to be an orphan, no-one was supposed to know who his parents had been. And who were *'the enemy'*? Just as Raza was thinking about these questions, the conversation continued.

The professor said, 'What about our clever friend, Raza, do we have any information on him?'

Raza froze at the sound of his own name.

Nina replied, 'We are getting closer, sir. He may not be from Afghanistan, he is more likely to be linked with Iran. That's as far as we have got, but his genes and DNA are interesting.'

Raza's mouth opened. For all of his life he had been told that he was from Afghanistan. To hear what had just been said seemed impossible.

The professor continued in his serious tone.

'Well, it doesn't matter too much. Raza is clearly an exceptional talent and his close friendship with Barry will be an enormous advantage if they become a team working for us. It would be good to know where our Raza comes from, but it's not essential.'

The professor's voice was very different to the one he had used the night before when talking to the new students. This morning his voice was very business-like. It was not warm and welcoming at all. It was cool and calculating.

'Russell, get the emergency procedures practised and done. We cannot take any chances at this stage and if we can just fool our enemies into leaving this area and searching somewhere else, we can all sleep easier at night. We will talk again at the same time tomorrow. Until then, we have twenty-one very special young people to introduce to our school and its amazing grounds. Good morning.'

Before Raza could hear Russell and Nina respond to this, he was gone. Back in his room, he sat on his bed and put his very bright, but at the moment, very confused mind to understanding what he had just heard.

At about 7.45, he could hear Barry moving around next door. Raza left his room and knocked on Barry's door. Barry opened the door and invited his friend into his room.

'Raza, how good is this? Did you get the message on the TV and gentle wake-up call?'

'No, Barry, I have been awake since 6am and I have walked all around the school already, while you have continued to dream and snore like a pig.' Raza knew the insult would give him more time to avoid having to discuss what he had seen and, more importantly, overheard outside the professor's office. He needed time to come to terms with the news before he shared it with anyone, even Barry.

'Now, Raza, we both know who snores around here and it isn't me!' replied Barry with a smile.

'Are you calling me a pig, Spotter?'

'What if I am, Hassan Raza, what if I am?'

With that, Raza launched himself at Barry and the two of them bounced onto the bed, each pulling at the head of the other, trying to get a headlock.

'Take it back or die, Spotter,' hissed Raza.

'I will die then, Raza, but not until I have heard you beg for mercy,' said Barry.

As the two continued to wrestle and squeal and laugh and make threats of great menace, the TV – and a voice on it – suddenly interrupted. It was Luigi.

'Breakfast isa ready. I 'ava lots a gooda theengs for you to a starta your firsta day 'ere.'

The boys let go of the hold they had on each other, each telling the other that he had been very lucky to live long enough for breakfast, and they made for the door, not wanting to be last again!

'Bet it's porridge, bet it's bacon and eggs,' they argued and made their way to the dining room, which was already busy with their new classmates who were either choosing or eating their breakfast.

There was freshly-squeezed orange juice, loads of fruit, all manner of cereals, meats, eggs cooked in various ways – scrambled, poached, fried – and even some pancakes with honey and lemon juice. The children just helped themselves. In these early days, it was important for the children to eat well and, for many of them, to make up for the poor diet that they had endured for most of their childhood. Towards the end of the meal, Russell spoke to them all.

'I hope you all slept well and that you have had plenty to eat. We will gather in the meeting circle at eight-thirty and then your tour of the school and its grounds will begin. The weather is good, so no special clothing is needed and the ground outside is dry, so come as you are. See you all at 8.30.'

Russell and Nina and several other adults, who had not yet been introduced to the children, left the dining room. At 8.30am precisely they and all the students assembled in the meeting circle. Russell spoke to the whole group.

'We will now begin our tour of the school and its grounds. When we come to individual classrooms, I will introduce you to the teachers who usually work in them with you. Do we have any questions?'

He looked at the group; there were no hands up. 'Right then, let's begin,' he said, and led the way down the corridor away from their rooms towards the professor's office. Of course, Raza had seen all this before, but he did not give anything away. As children gasped at the classrooms and the equipment inside them, he joined in so that no-one would have known that he had been there before. With his photographic memory, Raza was already sure of the layout of the school.

As they came to individual classrooms, Russell explained how they were used and who used them.

The room with headphones and kiosks was known as the language laboratory.

'In here, you will learn very quickly to speak French, German and Spanish. As the professor told you the other day, some of you will go on to learn Arabic, Russian, Chinese and other languages. The main teachers in here are Madame Leblanc and Senior Alphonse this year, but other teachers will come and go as the new languages are introduced.'

The two teachers came forward and smiled at the group. Madame Leblanc was an elegant lady wearing very smart clothes. She was young for a teacher and very pretty. When she smiled, her eyes and face lit up. Senior Alphonse was a dark-skinned little man. He had jet black hair that shone with health. He had a small beard and moustache. As the group moved on, Senior Alphonse caught Barry's eye and winked at him very quickly and secretly, and then followed the wink with a huge smile. Barry was impressed. These teachers seemed to have a sense of fun about them and he couldn't wait to get to their lessons and see if his ideas were right.

Next was the fitness room. This was a large room with lots of apparatus, such as exercise bikes, treadmills for running on, weights machines and technical equipment for measuring pulse rates and oxygen uptake. The two teachers in here were both dressed in tracksuits. They were introduced as Mr. Armstrong and Miss Dean.

'Would you like to do a bit of a demonstration for us? It can get a bit boring just looking into classrooms,' asked Russell.

The two teachers responded. Miss Dean began with a little run into a series of back flips and finished with a back somersault, landing perfectly and finishing with a little bow to the students, who gazed with mouths open at her skill.

Mr. Armstrong reached forward and slipped effortlessly into a headstand. He then pushed up into a handstand and then back to a headstand and up again into a handstand. As he did so, his muscles seemed to grow and stand out as if they had been blown up like a balloon. All the children gasped at first and then clapped loudly.

Next was the science room. In here, there were gas taps, sinks, fume cupboards and other cupboards full of strange apparatus which the children had never seen before. The science teacher was Mr. Gibbon. He had been one of the people in the 'Wonder Bus' on the day of the interviews, wearing a white coat. He had prepared for the first visit of the new pupils.

In front of him, he had a massive glass bowl of red water. Next to this was a tall glass jar with a glass lid on the top. It appeared to be empty.

'Good morning, scientists,' he said. The children all looked doubtful.

'You will all be scientists by the time you leave, believe me. Here at St. Gianeco's we do fascinating, exciting science. Just watch.'

Then he placed a small piece of white stuff, about the size of a pea, onto the red liquid. Immediately the substance began to fizz around the top of the liquid and a small flame and smoke appeared. The children stared in wonder. Then they noticed that the red liquid was changing to blue. Eventually, after a minute or two, the fizzing stopped and the children again clapped the performance.

'Not quite finished yet,' said Mr. Gibbon.

'What changes did you notice after I put the substance into the red water? Yes, that's all it was, coloured water.'

Émile said, 'It went blue, there was a flame, it hissed, it went in circles.' He was unable to hold his enthusiasm.

'All good observations, well done, Émile. Anything else?' asked Mr. Gibbon.

There was silence.

Barry broke the silence.

'I think some kind of fumes or gases were given off, but I'm not sure, because it had no colour.'

'Excellent, Barry, a colourless gas was given off and I have collected some of that gas in the tall jar here. Now watch this.'

He then lit a small, thin piece of wood and placed it into the jar.

Immediately there was a blue flame which seemed to slide down the jar and then there was a loud 'pop' as it reached the bottom and disappeared.

'In our first lesson together, you will be able to do just what I have done and I will explain to you what has happened. It will be your first chemistry lesson and you will all learn to love chemistry, that is my promise to you.'

As the children moved on, they did not doubt that they would learn to love chemistry. If it was as exciting and as much fun as what they had just seen, chemistry and science in general were going to be fantastic!

Barry looked at Raza as they moved on.

'Impressive,' said Raza, 'very impressive. I will try and find out about what we have just watched. Chemistry will be one of my strong subjects.'

He said this with absolute confidence. He was 'hooked' by what he had just seen, and Raza rarely changed his mind.

'Me too,' said Barry. 'That was great.'

The group continued to move on, meeting teachers, looking into rooms and then finally reaching the martial arts room.

In here an older man, dressed in a white karate suit, waited and silently met the eye of each of the children in turn. There was something a little strange about this small Japanese man and something that said you had to respect and obey him.

His hair was long and his eyes were steady. He seemed to never blink, his eyes just stared and seemed to take everything in.

'Good morning, new students. I am Mr. Shakitu. I look forward to teaching you to become some of the best martial arts pupils in the country. I will teach karate, judo, jujitsu and others. By the time you leave here, you will be highly trained in self-defence and you will never have to fear attack from anyone.

'I would like to show you a Kata that we will work on in our first lesson together.'

He then took up a fighting position and went through a sequence of moves, kicks and punches, which had the children spellbound. He grunted and shouted and almost screamed at some stages. It was a breathtaking performance. Afterwards, he stood for a second and bowed to his pupils. Again they clapped. No smile found its way onto Mr. Shakito's face, only a look of total dedication, strength and courage. Russell and the other adults with the group bowed respectfully and then the group moved on in silence. Mr. Shakito had put on an awesome display.

From here the group passed through the glass doors to a large hall at the back of the school. Here hung the magnificent Second World War fighter plane, the 'Hurricane'. Again, as others looked and marvelled at this fabulous little plane, Raza said nothing about his visit here earlier in the day.

Eventually the group went through another set of doors to look at the school grounds, where other amazing sights awaited them.

The children left the school building below the level of the fake reservoir or lake, and a bank of grass went up from the doors to the top of the reservoir.

'Right then, let's see who can be first to the top of this bank?' said Russell. The children ran and shouted up the hill and when they got there they saw something quite strange.

There was no water at all on the surface, but there was a space of about one metre between the top of the bank and the glass that formed the roof of the school below and, at the same time, the bottom of the fake lake. Coming out of the sides were some pipes. Barry looked at these and tried to work out why the pipes were there and why there was this space between the top of the bank and the school's glass roof.

'What are the pipes for, Russell?' asked Barry.

'They are water pipes Barry, we use them to clean the glass roof and occasionally for other things, which I won't go into just now.'

As Russell said this, there was something wrong with the tone of his voice and the look on his face, suggesting that he was not giving the children the full story, but holding something back. Barry and Raza shared a look that said they had both noticed this answer as being not completely true. Gianeco's had its secrets, of that they were both sure!

Russell spoke to them all.

'Now turn and look away from the reservoir.'

As the new students turned, they gasped.

Below them was a forest. A forest that was thick and green.

These children had all come from towns and cities, and to look out on all this space and these trees just took their breath away. They stared and pointed and stared some more.

Russell explained, 'The school grounds go as far as you can see, almost a mile in all directions. At the very edge, which we can't even see from here, is a high wire fence. So you cannot get totally lost and no-one from outside the school can come into the grounds. We have cameras in various places around the grounds just to make sure. Out there in the forest you will find small ponds, streams, dark places, places to pitch a tent, cycle tracks and, most importantly, something that I want to show you rather than tell you about. Just look down there to the right a little and watch.'

He put his hands to the sides of his mouth and shouted, 'OK, Nina, let's see you go!'

Suddenly from the tops of the trees in the distance came a figure, almost flying through the trees. The flying figure zig-zagged from tree to tree and finally landed on the ground where the forest finished, just by the entrance to the school. The figure waved to the students. They all waved and cheered back. It was Nina, and her smile shone up to them even from a distance.

Russell smiled and continued.

'The forest has cables and zip wires all through it. So when you travel through the forest, you can go on foot, on a bike, or through the tree tops like Nina just did. We will teach you how to use harnesses and safety equipment, of course, but you will all be able to use them safely within a day or two and then it's up to you!

'I guess you would like to see more of the grounds and try out our zip wires?' asked Russell.

'Let's go then, down the hill and into the forest.'

The children raced down the grass bank, some fell and tumbled, others decided to roll down anyway and eventually they met with Nina. The whole group ran into the forest, until they came to the start of a zip wire. At the bottom of the tree was a set of brand new mountain bikes.

'At each zip wire base or station, you will find bikes like these. You can use them whenever you like as long as you leave them at a station – not the same one, of course, but any of the stations throughout the forest. This is how we all get around the grounds. Some of you can have a ride now if you like, try them out. Who is first to go on the zip wire then?'

Immediately some children took to the bikes and the others lined up to be fitted with safety harnesses ready for their first go on the zip wires.

After an hour or two, when all the children had had at least three turns on a zip wire, ridden the bikes and generally had a great time, Russell asked them to sit on the grass. Two of the chefs brought out drinks and a few biscuits and, as the children munched and drank, Russell spoke to them again.

'So you see, St. Gianeco's is special inside and outside. There are lots of other things in the grounds. We have an artificial ski slope, swimming pool, fishing lakes and lots more. What you have seen is enough for one day. In a minute we will leave you all to just look around, to play, to ride bikes and climb trees. You can do anything you want to do, as long as you are careful. But, before I go, there is one very important noise that you have to recognise and respond to immediately if you hear it.

'We call it our emergency procedures siren. When you hear it, you have two minutes to get into school or, if you are out in the grounds, to get into a covered place, under a tree or somewhere else dark and not visible from above.'

He looked at the children and his face had changed. Russell was now very serious and quite scary to look at. He took his time and looked at each of the children in turn.

'It is absolutely vital that you all obey this order. If you do not, you will be expelled from this school. There are no second chances. Your safety depends on this.' He looked around as all the children nodded in silence.

'Now, this is the trial. You must do as I have just said and wait for the siren to sound for a second time, which means that the emergency is over. Are you ready?'

Russell then signalled towards the school and the loudest, most frightening siren that ever sounded, went off. The children covered their ears as the sound pierced the air..

Russell shouted, 'Now run for the forest and find somewhere covered, dark and safe. Go!'

The children ran as if in fear of their lives and soon they began to stop and hide and curl up, afraid of something they did not know or understand. After a minute or two Russell and Nina began to move through the trees and as they did they praised the children for finding such good hiding places. 'Well done, Emile.' 'Good place, Gemma,' they said.

After a few more minutes, the two adults began to look worried again.

'Where are Barry and Raza?' Russell asked.

'Barry, Raza, where are you? Come out, it's safe now, where are you?'

But there was no sign of the two boys.

'Barry! Raza!' All the children called.

Still there was no sign of the two boys.

Russell and Nina now became very worried. The first day and they had lost two students already.

'Raza, Barry, come on now, it's over, it's all safe. The test is finished, come out,' Nina shouted. There was still no sign of them.

'The professor will go mad; day one, two children lost and it was only a test of the emergency siren,' said Russell.

'I have an idea,' said Nina, 'sound the siren again.'

'What? Why?' said Russell.

'Just do it!' said Nina in a very stern voice.

Russell waved to the school and the siren very briefly sounded again.

As the siren sounded, two thuds were heard and two boys, Barry and Raza, appeared from nowhere!

'What! How the hell..? Where were you?' shrieked Russell. He was relieved and shocked at the same time.

'Why didn't you come out just now when I shouted?'

Barry looked at Raza and then said, 'Because you said the emergency was not over until we heard the siren again. You said that we would be expelled from here if we broke the rule. Raza and I don't want to be expelled, so we stayed up in the tree until we heard the siren.'

He looked at Russell, who at first seemed a little angry, but then he looked at Nina and both of them and the other children all broke into laughter. Barry and Raza just smiled; they did not see the joke!

CHAPTER 18

Solving the First Mystery

That evening, after dinner, Barry and Raza went to their rooms. After about an hour Barry heard a knock on his door. He opened the door and found Raza.

'Come in, Raz, I am just on the computer looking at the websites on planes, the Spitfire and the Hurricane.'

'Did you know, Raza, that the Spitfire was designed by a man called Reginald Mitchell from Stoke-on-Trent?'

Raza looked at Barry, impressed with his friend's growing knowledge.

'No, Baz, I didn't, but I do now!' said Raza.

They both went to the computer and began to read the information together.

'Interesting, Baz, but would you like to learn something really interesting?'

'Like what, brainbox?' said Barry.

Raza looked at Barry. Normally he would have grabbed him at this stage and begun a fight, but tonight he had more important things to share with Barry.

'No fights tonight, Baz, we need to use both our brains to work some things out.'

Barry stared at his friend. He had not seen him so serious since the day at the comprehensive school when they had been bullied so badly.

Raza went to the door, opened it and checked that no-one was listening. He then returned and sat on Barry's bed.

'Barry,' he said. 'Are you happy here?'

'Raz, what sort of question is that? Of course I am, it's the best place in the world. Why, are you unhappy? What's wrong?'

'Oh no, Baz! This **is** the best place in the world. For me it is perfect. I can learn any number of languages, self-defence, chemistry and maybe even to fly. I can ride zip wires until I'm daft and I have my best friend in the world next door to me. Of course I am happy.'

'So what is behind your question, Raz?'

'Barry, I am happy, but I am puzzled. There are lots of questions about this place that are in my head. There are things I want to tell you, so you will see what I mean.'

'Don't scare me, Raza, what is it I need to know? This sounds worrying to me.' The fear was never far away, and Useless' words kept coming back to Barry in quiet moments.

'Barry, this morning when I was walking around the school I heard Nina, Russell and the professor talking. They were talking about **you** mostly and a bit about me.'

'That will teach you to listen to other people's conversations, Raza. Don't be a snoop.'

'Barry, I was not snooping, I just overheard a conversation.'

Barry looked unconvinced; he knew his friend too well!

'OK, I was snooping! BUT, listen to this and don't get all weird on me when I tell you something.'

'Go on then, tell me something interesting, Raza.'

'They – the professor, Nina and Russell – know who your parents were, they know where you come from and they have done DNA tests to prove it.'

It took time for this to sink in, but eventually Barry managed to speak.

'You are sure that they know who my parents were and they have not told me?' asked Barry.

'Exactly, Barry, that's one question. But I also heard them say that your parents were special and that's the reason you were chosen for this place. Think about it, Barry. Out of thousands of kids, we were chosen. Two orphans along with nineteen other orphans. What makes us so special?' Raza looked hard at his friend.

'Well, your parents make you special and that's why you are here.'

Barry thought about this for a while and then asked,

'OK, that's me explained, what about you, Raza? Why are you here?'

'I'm here because of you, Barry. Because you would not come without me and they had to have you here. It was always their plan, they have searched for you in loads of children's homes and at last they found you at Freeman's . And I will always be grateful to you, my best friend. Because of you, I will realise my dreams and I will learn the things I want so much to learn.'

Barry replied, 'Raza, I would not be here if you were not, because you are like my brother. We will never be separated. We both know that.'

Raza continued, 'I heard the three of them say that they did not know anything about my parents, but I may come from Iran – not Afghanistan, as I have always believed. You see, Barry, so many questions and here are some more.

'One, why did we have the emergency training today? What do we have to fear?

'Two, why was Nina so scared of the helicopter? I heard them talking about that today as well.'

'What did they say, Raza?' Barry asked this with his eyes fixed on those of his friend. This conversation was getting very serious.

'They said that it was probably their enemies in the helicopter. Why would a school have **enemies**, Barry?

Three, why did the professor look so sneaky when I asked him who Gianeco Leapos was?'

'Raza, you are scaring me now. What is all this, why can't we just enjoy ourselves here?'

'Barry, you know as well as I do that we have to know the answers to these questions. And I have left the best until last.'

'Oh, go on, Raz, scare me some more. What else have you discovered?'

Raza gave Barry his most serious look and then said, 'I have searched the internet since we arrived, Barry, and there is no record of any Saint Gianeco Leapos. There is nothing in the Greek history or religion to suggest that he ever existed!'

'Oh great, Raz, so they just invented the name, is that it?'

'Yes, Barry, I am convinced that they invented the name Gianeco Leapos, and that it is an anagram. The letters are mixed up, but if you put them in the right order, you will find something else perhaps.'

'So you think that maybe hidden in the letters is a real name for this school?'

'Yes, Barry, and I have started to work it out, but I cannot discover the answer just yet. We need to work on it together. I need your help.'

'Raza, if you are right, we could discover the secret name, and if we do, this name might answer some of the other questions you have just asked.'

'Tomorrow we have the morning off to explore the forest. You and I will take some paper and pens and work on this puzzle in the forest. We always work best in the fresh air!'

Both boys slept badly that night. Their heads were full of questions and ideas for solving the riddle of 'St. Gianeco Leapos'. After breakfast Barry and Raza made their way into the forest. At first they could hear voices of other children, but then after a while they were all alone. They sat on some fallen logs by a stream and started to work on the anagram.

STGIANECOLEAPOS

They worked on separate pieces of paper at first.

'Just take out words first of all, Raza,' said Barry. 'Any words.' So they began.

BEST

NOSE

BASE

GLEE

ANGELS

ANGLES

ABLE

SAGE

STOOGE

BASIS

STAGE

NESTS

SENSIBLE

'These are all good words, Raza, but it's not getting us any closer to solving the anagram. Maybe it's two words or three that we are looking for. Let's try again.'

So they began again, searching for words that just might throw some light on the real name of their new and exciting school, using the name of the saint that had never existed.

Then it happened. The first breakthrough and it was Barry who got it.

'Raz, Raz, I think I have one of the words. Look! Look here.' And there it was, one of the words they were looking for:

AGENTS.

'Agents, Raza, we are training to become agents.'

'Well done, Baz, now let's take out those letters and see what we are left with.' And they did. The letters were:

ISCOLEAPOS

They began again:
   POLE,

   POSE

   LEAPS

   SLOPE

Then Raza shouted, 'Got it, well almost, I think. Look, Barry.' And there it was, the second word.

SPECIAL

'*Special agents* academy. *Special agents* academy, that's got to be it. They are training us to be come spies, Barry. Special agents, spies!'

'Hang on, Raza, what about the two other letters? We are now left with two 'o's, we haven't used them yet.'

'Let's just think about this a bit more, Raz.' And they did. Then Barry smiled.
   'What are you smiling at, Barry? We have not cracked it yet.'
   'Oh, we have, Raza, oh yes we have.'
   'Tell me then, how have we have cracked the anagram with two 'o's left over?'
   'That's because they aren't 'o's, Raza, they are zeros; numbers not letters! And what do all British special agents have as well as their names, Raza?'
   Raza had no answer.
   'Raza, they have a number and that number begins with 00, zero, zero, but we say 'o-o', like when people give out telephone numbers they do the same.' The two boys sat for a while just taking in what they had discovered.

Barry broke the silence.
   'We are being trained to become special agents. That's why we need to learn other languages, self-defence, flying lessons and all the other great things we are going to learn here!'
   'Now it begins to make sense and that's why we have enemies, people who want to know where the next lot of special agents are being trained!'

The two boys fell silent. There was a lot to take in. After a few minutes they looked at each other, and smiled and high-fived!

'So what do you want to do now, Baz? Do we go to the professor and tell him, or see Nina and Russell and tell them what we think we have discovered?' asked Raza.

'I don't think so, Raz. There is really only one important and proper thing to do at a time like this.'

They looked to their left, and both of them saw what they wanted to see. They both ran like mad men and yelled at the top of their voices, 'ZIP WIRE!!!'

THE END OF PART ONE

Lightning Source UK Ltd.
Milton Keynes UK
UKOW051527300112

186333UK00001B/73/P